When You Find Us
We Will Be Gone

When You Find Us We Will Be Gone

Christopher Linforth

LAMAR UNIVERSITY press

ISBN: 978-0-9911074-9-0
Library of Congress Control Number: 2014940574

Manufactured in the United States
Book Design: Crystal M. Smith
Cover Design: Alban Fischer

Lamar University Press
Beaumont, Texas

For M

Other Books from Lamar University Press

Jean Andrews, *High Tides, Low Tides: the Story of Leroy Colombo*
Alan Berecka, *With Our Baggage*
David Bowles, *Flower, Song, Dance: Aztec and Mayan Poetry*
Jerry Bradley, *Crownfeathers and Effigies*
Robert Murray Davis, *Levels of Incompetence: An Academic Life*
William Virgil Davis, *The Bones Poems*
Jeffrey DeLotto, *Voices Writ in Sand*
Gerald Duff, *Memphis Mojo*
Mimi Ferebee, *Wildfires and Atmospheric Memories*
Ken Hada, *Margaritas and Redfish*
Michelle Hartman, *Disenchanted and Disgruntled*
Gretchen Johnson, *The Joy of Deception and Other Stories*
Gretchen Johnson, *A Trip Through Downer, Minnesota*
Lynn Hoggard, *Motherland, Stories and Poems from Louisiana*
Dominique Inge, *A Garden on the Brazos*
Tom Mack and Andrew Geyer, eds, *A Shared Voice*
Janet McCann, *The Crone at the Casino*
Erin Murphy, *Ancilla*
Dave Oliphant, *The Pilgrimage, Selected Poems: 1962-2012*
Harold Raley, *Louisiana Rogue*
Carol Coffee Reposa, *Underground Musicians*
Jim Sanderson, *Trashy Behavior*
Jan Seale, *Appearances*
Jan Seale, *The Parkinson Poems*
Carol Smallwood, *Water, Earth, Air, Fire, and Picket Fences*
Melvin Sterne, *The Number You Have Reached*

www.LamarUniversityPress.Org

Acknowledgments

My endless gratitude goes to the editors of the journals in which versions of these stories first appeared:

C4 Magazine
Chicago Quarterly Review
Gargoyle
Harpur Palate
Hawaii Pacific Review
The Lindenwood Review
Lunch Ticket
The MacGuffin
Phantom Drift
Red Earth Review
Southern Humanities Review
Swarm

Also, my deepest thanks to Lucinda Roy, Ed Falco, Matthew Vollmer, Fred D'Aguiar, and the graduate students at Virginia Tech; to my friends; to Maria Stack; to Jerry Craven and his staff at Lamar University Press; and to the Virginia Center for the Creative Arts for the time to revise many of the stories.

CONTENTS

Homeland

Saskia waits for me at the airport, cup of *bijela kava* in one hand and a cigarette in the other, yet she seems impatient, unsatisfied. Later, in the warmth of her sheets, this image of her still strikes me as troubling, even as I roll out of her bed and take a piss in the bathroom down the hall. She shares the apartment with Colin, an architect from Ireland. He loves Croatia, especially the city life of Zagreb. The people, he tells me time and time again, share the same spirit of rebellion. He argues both countries are perennial underdogs, always will be. The British were his oppressors; the Serbs for the Croats. As I fetch a glass of water from the kitchen, I want to forget about Colin and his cultural analysis. I want Saskia to live with me in D.C. I have never been happy with her sharing an apartment with a man. He works out and likes to roam the place in his black silk boxers and play his Martin guitar through the night. Saskia joins in, sings "The Bold Fenian Men," and dances around the living room.

In her bedroom, she opens one eye and looks at me—scanning my potbelly and gray hair at the temples. I feel all of my forty-two years. She's a decade younger, her body thin and muscular. Her honey-colored skin and natural blond hair appear unaffected by her chain-smoking and short sleeping hours. Sometimes I barely know her at all, and I think this is because of the age difference. We met on a reconstruction project eighteen months after the war. My job was to facilitate the rebuilding of the electrical grid. Several power plants had been crippled by JNA artillery and aerial bombardment. She worked as a translator, coordinating the paperwork and liaising between the Croatian government and the company I worked for. Our meetings blossomed into dates and then a long-distance relationship that has been atrophying for the last seven years.

"Alexander," she says. She's the only one who calls me this. To everyone else it is Alex. "Can I have it?"

1

I pass her the glass and slide back into bed. Her fluency in English has always thrown me, kept me off-guard. She can slip between languages, navigating complex ideas with more insight than I could ever muster. She studied French literature at Sveučilište u Zagrebu and then completed an intensive summer course at the Sorbonne. She worships Voltaire and Sartre and likes to quote from *Candide* or *Huis Clos* at dinner or on our walks. For her coursework she wrote long analytical essays on notions of the real in Zola, and she now keeps the papers stacked on her nightstand, pinned by a statuette of Marianne. Saskia has the mind of the philosopher, an existentialist forever questioning meaning. She once told me she learned Italian in her *gimnazija* in order to claim Dalmatia back. By disentangling the language from the land, she would be able to discover the purity that existed before the invasion. I know she would like to do the same thing for Serbian, but the languages are too similar, and I have seen her say *Josip Jović* in pain.

"Do you want to go out for breakfast?" she says.

"I have a meeting," I say. The project I have worked on all these years is coming to an end. Soon there will be no reason for me to be in the country. Saskia knows this, yet has offered no thoughts on me leaving for good.

She snorts and wraps herself in the sheets. "Say hi to Tomislav for me."

* * *

I drive Saskia's Yugo from her tower block in the east section of Novi Zagreb to the center of the city. In the crisp November light the concrete buildings are thrown into sharp contrast—rectangular outlines flat as monoliths dominate the skyline. Near the river I hear the clanging of the tram and see, as it turns the corner, old women staring out from the dirt-smudged windows. It has been three months since I was last here. My job requires tri-annual visits, each lasting a month at a time. Our relationship is built on these tenuous periods. We eat out a lot, drink *pivo* and *rakija*, talk with her friends. They seem enthralled with the new Croatia, a country on the edge of Europe but not allowed in it. They barely mention the fall of Communism, the name *Tito* a distant memory, a fragment that still scares their parents. They don't think much of Bush or America, viewing the country as colonizers, *slijepi* warmongers. Sometimes I reason this is why Saskia has not ventured to D.C. She says her job keeps her busy all of the year. There's distrust, a sense I am trying to take her away.

In Tomislav's office, I sit and wait for him to arrive. He has never approved of my and Saskia's relationship. He was jealous, wanted her for himself. We are of a similar age and he has a wife now, from Karlovac, though I frequently mispronounce her name.

"Alex," he says, entering. His tone is warm, and, as I stand, he shakes my hand. "Good to see you again."

"Likewise."

He looks the same: his dark double-breasted suit, taupe T-shirt, and a gold curb-link chain just visible around the bottom of his neck. When I first met him, he took me out to shoot a game of pool, and, after I beat him, he challenged me to an arm wrestle. That night he introduced me to Saskia, said she was his assistant. He groped her knee in the darkness of the bar, and she looked away unable to make eye contact with either of us. Then he had children—Marko, Jelena, Renata—and quit drinking. He blamed his past behavior on his youth, on the fact he needed a woman to translate for him.

On my computer I run through charts detailing contingency plans for the electrical grid, but I keep thinking of Saskia in bed and Colin in the room next door. She has told me on several occasions she doesn't find him attractive, that she finds his near-nakedness funny and his accent engaging—like a lost troubadour finding his way in the world. She rarely speaks about me in those terms, or even says what she thinks of me; what she admires or hates.

"Are you well?" asks Tomislav.

I nod, and carry on, sleepwalking through the PowerPoint. I click through the slides of the latest efficiency improvements at the Peruća dam. The concrete rampart was cracked by JNA explosives and threatened a dozen small villages in the lower valley. It took years for Hrvatska Elektroprivreda to re-start power generation. I talk of the possible future developments and then, after I am finished, he passes me a handful of documents and I check them over and slip them into my briefcase.

3

"I'll get these authorized and then we're set," I say. "Done."

"It has been good working with you," says Tomislav.

"Hard to believe all the years that have passed."

"What will you do next?"

"There are several projects in India," I say, standing. "I don't know. We'll see."

"Good luck," he says, showing me to the door. "And tell Saskia if she ever wants her job back..."

I block out his words, but the sound of his voice lingers—even as I exit the building. Saskia confessed in the early days of our dating that she had slept with Tomislav, that she felt forced to in order to keep her job. Neither of us brought it up again. In the car, I rest my head on the steering wheel. The Yugo insignia on the column has been stickered over with a map of France. I peel it off, smell the cheap glue on the reverse, and glance at the two crooked lines that form a Y. I replace the sticker, press it down hard with a flattened palm. On the way back, I stop at a kiosk to buy glossy postcards of the Well of Life and the Ethnographic Museum, cheap versions of my memories. In one of the exhibition halls, as we indulged in the folk costumes, I had given Saskia a chance. Said I would move in with her. She told me to focus on my career, for she was not worth the sacrifice.

* * *

Saskia's on the balcony, smoking a cigarette and eating black cherries. Maria Callas croons from the portable stereo by her feet. I imagine Saskia's thinking of me, and what she's going to do once I leave. My flight departs in the morning. No month this time. Soon I am going to be living in my row house in Tenleytown, pacing through the neighborhood, checking my messages, and occasionally gawking at the exchange students at AU, wondering if any of them are from the Balkans.

I press my face against the glass door, trying to get a better view. Colin is resting in a deckchair on the far side of the balcony. He holds a beer and a cellphone in one hand, while he swirls the other in the air to reinforce his joke about Bush's resemblance to an ape. He delivers an obvious punch line, and she laughs. I tap on the glass.

"Alexander," she says, turning. "How was the meeting?"

4

I crack open the door. "I'm about to pack."

"Stay," she says, "have a cherry."

I shake my head and go to her room and toss my shirts into my suitcase. The postcards I sent her are tacked to the dresser drawers. She once said the White House looks funny, like an old plantation house. If she saw it in person, she would say it looks small—like everyone else. I keep the one letter she has written in my medicine cabinet, rolled tight in a plastic sleeve. When I see my reflection, I think of her and what she let slip. She sent me the letter a week after I first left and wrote of a book historicizing the romance of the theologian Abélard and his student Héloïse. In her scrawl I learned that Héloïse's uncle castrated Abélard for wanting to marry the girl. She became a nun; he a monk. For the rest of their lives they communicated through letters. For two pages Saskia deliberated on the romance and underlined a sentence about *unity in distance*. She argued our time apart strengthened us, kept us together. I was never convinced and pleaded for a little leeway. She allowed me weekly telephone calls and e-mails, though no other letters. I have flown in for multiple visits, saving my flextime to spend long weekends with her. She used to relish these short stays, but over the last months she told me to save my money and spend it on something else.

Saskia knocks softly on the door and comes in. "Are you all right?" Her brow is wrinkled, and her left hand touches her lips.

"Fine." I fold my suit in half and throw it into the case.

She steps closer and caresses my shoulder. "What was *that* back there?"

"Nothing."

"We should talk about it."

"Where do we go from here?"

She looks down at the hardwood. "I don't know."

This is the first time I have seen self-doubt in her. Usually she's confident, like nothing can touch her. That every word she says is the way it is.

"I was waiting until you left," she says, "to see how I really feel."

I don't understand why she still is unsure. Saskia is so different from the other women I have known. Anya, the girlfriend prior, was a Peace Corps volunteer. She built a school in Angola and then taught English. I

5

let her go—wanted her to earn her Ph.D. Then there was Elizabeth, my college girlfriend. At William and Mary she was a psychology major who wanted to become a behavioral counselor. We assumed we would marry post-graduation. She changed, or I did, in D.C., the city too much to bear. Sometimes I blame myself, my propensity to romanticize and ignore my own failings. I try to rationalize Saskia's behavior in my head, relate it to her father killed in the war and her mother drunk on *domaća šljivovica*. But no. I have met many women over here who want to settle down, start a family, make a life after all the bloodshed.

"O.K.," I say. "I need to finish packing."

She slips out of the room, and I sit on the foot of the bed. I am not sure how this situation has come to pass. Over the years, I have worked myself up from an assistant project manager to executive. Yet our roles have reversed. I am consigned to be her inferior. Each action she completes is on a higher order and mysteriously imbued with meaning. She leaves me deciphering, trying to ascertain what to do next.

* * *

When Saskia asks me to go with her to the market, I agree. How can I not? It's located a few streets down from her apartment and we walk, side by side. Her hands are sunk in her woolen overcoat, probably so that she doesn't have to hold mine. It's strange. I like her clothes. She has an offbeat style: mud-brown corduroys, cork-heeled wedges, a purple scarf loosely wrapped around her neck and over her right shoulder. I rarely break from my dark suits and white cotton shirts. My tie, though, sits squashed in my pocket. I caress the silk as we hook a right onto a concrete plaza jostling with people navigating the stalls. Produce vendors, women from the countryside outside of Zagreb, cry out, encouraging people to buy their homemade cheeses and flatbreads. In the center of the market stands a bronze statue of King Tomislav riding a horse. The marble base is scrawled with graffiti, and a group of teenagers leans against the slab.

"How did your meeting go?" she says.

"The usual," I note. "He looks good."

"Really?"

"When was the last time you saw him?"

"A while ago," she says, pointing to one of the stalls. "I want quince."

"I thought we were getting food for dinner?"

"Fine," she says, and leads me to a man selling grains pooled in plastic buckets.

I buy five-hundred grams of wheat flour to make dumplings.

"Chicken," she notes. "We need some."

We head to a stall, find trays of butchered meat, and I pull out my wallet and count my remaining kuna.

"Saskia, what about these?" I turn and she's gone. I think I see her through the crowd. Sloping away. I shake my head and purchase a handful of chicken thighs, enough to make a rich soup. Her mother taught me the recipe on the second day I met her. I don't think she remembers the first. A Christmas years ago Saskia coaxed me onto a train heading east to Slavonia, to a rural town close to the Serbian border. The carriages were full of grizzled men smoking and arguing over the exact position where Croatia ends and other places begin. In a taxi to the house, she told me what the men had said and that the men were stupid for fighting over the land. Her mother was in the yard with a tall glass of *šljivovica* in her hand and standing over a pig roasting on an iron spit. After she kissed me on the cheek and learned my name, saying it slowly three times, she ripped a hunk of bread from a large circular loaf and dipped it in the liquid pig fat caught in the silver foil below the carcass. She handed the sodden bread to me and laughed as I coughed up the salty dough.

In America, I am rarely that daring; I spend my days avoiding new experiences. I focus on my job, the planning of sustainable Third World electrical grids. I rethink the infrastructure, shifting the energy mix from crumbling coal plants to wind farms, hydroelectric dams, and nuclear installations. I demand backup generators in hospitals, and I pilot residential microgrids in the favelas. I help people. I power the homes of families. Makes my life feel it is worth a damn. Perhaps in a small way this makes up for Bush. It is a strange kind of delusion, one that keeps me going. When I am here, with Saskia, her friends treat me like an oddity. They invite me to cafés, encourage me to drink and smoke, to relax and forget about work. They recount stories of sexual misdeeds, and hurl *Ti si šupak* and *Idi u kurac* at each other, and in their whispers I hear fragmented critiques of both Communist rule and capitalism. I feel serene,

7

above the words, like a U.N. observer. A stranger who can barely navigate the peculiarities of translation, and yet I hope when the right words can't be found they see the good in me, the foreigner. And when Saskia's cold, she will remember what I first said to her in the bar and come around. Take me back. I wrestle with my faith in her, in us, on the walk to the apartment. Colin lets me in. He's wearing an emerald-green kimono, a swirling black dragon embroidered on the back.

"You look like shit," he says, grins.

I step inside, think at least I don't sing like it, and begin to put the groceries away. He comes into the kitchen, maneuvers around me, and snatches a beer from the fridge.

"Is Saskia with you?" he asks.

"No."

"Sounds about right."

He doesn't wait for my reply. He goes to the living room, and I follow him to give him a better answer, to show him I am with her and that he isn't. He sits at the dining table, his laptop displaying the schematics of a modern industrial building.

"What's that?"

"Designs for a museum," he says, tapping his fingers on the screen, "to document the Homeland War."

"When will we see it?"

"I'm not sure it's going to be built. Bureaucracy is killing the funding."

"Life of an architect, I suppose."

Colin laughs. "Yeah, that's right."

"Saskia's at the market."

"Gotcha," he says, returning to the designs. "Grab a beer. I want to show you something."

"I'm good," I say, sideswiped by his warmth. "What is it?"

He loads up a three-dimensional image of the museum. With his mouse he rotates the building, clicks on the portico entrance, and zooms in. "The thing that kills me is I've spent longer on this project than anything else. Fucking years." He pokes his finger at his initials hidden in a stone recess. "I gave the place my mark."

"Maybe it's for the best," I say. "I mean, the country can move on from the war."

"Man, you don't understand Croats at all."

I don't want to think Colin's right, that he understands Saskia better than me. "I know about her father. That he was a police officer who fought the Serbs."

Colin mumbles a "Yeah." He's not looking at his computer anymore. He's looking at me.

"Killed," I add.

"And her brother," he says.

She never told me of a brother. Though, thinking back, I recall seeing a photograph in her room in Slavonia. He had a shock of dark hair and a thin face. I presumed he was an old boyfriend. "What was his name?"

"Stjepan."

"Stjepan," I repeat.

* * *

Saskia shows up after eight. Crescents underneath her eyes are tinged purple. She sweeps back her hair, wraps it with a blood-red kerchief, and touches my shoulder. She looks into my eyes, and I question what she's finding. She wants me to be angry, to chastise her for leaving.

"Hey," I say.

"I needed some time," she replies.

"Sure, I understand."

She guides me to the kitchen. We cook dinner as if nothing has happened. She has walked off before, told me she wanted a cigarette. Knows I don't like the smoke. But I don't remember her ever going for this long. Her hands look cold, almost blue. She says they're fine and boils the dumplings and chops the carrots and cabbage, while I prepare the chicken. I slice the flesh from the bone and cube the meat. As I pan-fry the chicken, I think about where she went, who she was with. She has a lot of male friends: Vladan, Ivan, Tomislav. I have met each of them over the years. Hated them all. Stjepan complicates things, makes me search for what else she hasn't told me. Maybe it's me, wanting her to open up my life.

I drop the chicken into the pot with the vegetables. I can hear Colin

9

in his room, playing his guitar. I switch on the TV; tell Saskia there's a news segment I want to watch. She laughs and says my Croatian is terrible, that I will not be able to understand what they are saying. She's right about my language skills. Being with her meant I didn't have to pick up that much. Still, I know one or two words. Early on I learnt how to say *volim te*, and in the first months I told her often. Saskia refused to reciprocate, said our relationship was different to love, transcended it.

We eat the dumplings and soup and drink a whole bottle of red wine. I pour Irish whisky into two tumblers and nudge her to the bedroom. Lying in bed, she unbuttons my shirt and runs her hand through my chest hair. She looks to the ceiling as she curls the black hairs between her fingers. She always liked doing this, calls me her grizzly bear.

"Found a gray," she says.

"Matches my hair."

She plucks the strand and rolls to the other side of the bed. "I have it now," she says.

I rub my chest, feeling the sting of the plucked follicle, and inch over to her. She's lined up at the edge, staring at her desk, or the college papers, or Marianne. I hook my arm around her waist and ask, "What are you going to do with it?"

"Pass my drink," she says.

"All right."

She's bored with the flirting, with me. We each drain our respective glasses and then, as I take her tumbler, she kisses my cheek.

"Don't you want to make love to me?"

She used to say *fuck*. Love is an acquiescence to me—a sign of regret, a mellowing of her sexual desire.

"I don't think it's right."

She whispers words of cryptic Croatian into my ear, her tongue tracing the contour of my lobe, and then she cups my face, angles it toward her. There's a slow meeting of our bodies. She latches us together with her limbs. They're limber, strong. Her hips grind mine for what seems like hours. The deep grooves on the inside of her legs bore into my body. I run my fingertips down her back and over the scars. She pushes my hands away and shakes her head. Lifting herself off me, she collapses onto her side of the bed. She has never explained these marks, and really I don't want to know.

10

* * *

I wake to see dark sky through the parting of loose curtain. Saskia's still asleep. I think about calling a taxi, not saying goodbye. I need a reason to keep the pain going or end the relationship for good. I nudge her shoulder and kiss her forehead. Her eyes stay closed. She smiles and throws her arm around my neck, kisses me on the lips. Her sour breath tastes of a last time.

She drives me to the airport in the creep of dusk. Her car struggles with the incline, and we can hear the hum of the trucks as they overtake us. Out of the window the scouring light reveals the jagged gray mountains on the horizon. I turn to her, place my hand on her knee and squeeze it gently. She stares forward, with hands unmoved in the two-and-ten position on the wheel. She's wearing a military overcoat and a pale yellow slip underneath. Her effortless beauty makes me jealous, makes me wonder. I am not sure what she does when I am in D.C., grinding through sixty-hour weeks. She says she translates government documents, goes out with friends to the bars on Tkalčićeva Street, devours the novels of Simone de Beauvoir, calls her mother and tries to understand how they have drifted apart.

The terminal comes into view, a large block of concrete and glass. She pulls into the parking lot and finds an empty space. She switches the engine off and unbuckles her seatbelt.

"You don't have to come in," I say.

"We should take a coffee," she replies.

"If you want."

"Of course I do."

"Will you tell me about Stjepan?"

She glares at me, trying to piece together how I found out. "Colin told you."

I nod.

She's quiet for a moment. Her face is flushed red. "He was shot."

"I'm sorry," I say. "I shouldn't have said anything."

"You're a fuck."

"I know."

"He was five years older than me. He taught me how to ride a horse.

He gave me my first cigarette," she says, clasping the handbag in her lap. "I remember him every day."

I want to thank her for sharing with me. But I know she would curse me out as American, all touchy-feely—constantly having to express.

She opens her door. "It's time."

We head inside the terminal. I show the attendant my passport and collect my ticket. We stop at the bar and get two cups of *bijela kava*. She lights a cigarette and inhales a long puff of gray smoke. She notices me watching her.

"I'm going to quit," she says.

I laugh. "Sure you are."

She squeezes my hand and tells me I should come back. I nod, not sure if I will. She doesn't seem affected by my response. She's prone to stoicism, to internalizing her emotions. She would just say she's being Slavic.

"By the next time you're here, I'll be free."

"Yeah, I know."

From her handbag she removes a book. She places it on the counter.

"A gift," she says.

It's a rare edition of *The Letters of Abélard and Héloïse*. I can't tell if this is meant to be symbolic of us parting or that it's a reminder we are still together.

"I'll read it onboard."

"Wait until you are home," she says.

"O.K."

We look out the large plate-glass windows and watch a plane land. I check the departure board. See that the numbers are orderly. She starts to talk about the flag on the rudder, what the design means, but I can only focus on the people swarming the gate.

The Cowboys of Fukushima

We were told the cows had gone feral, that in the days after the accident they had broken free of the pen and disappeared into the surrounding hills. Government officials were spooked by the rumors of this wild herd, declaring that the cattle posed a radiation risk to the elderly civilians still living in the warehouse on the outskirts of the city. On first meeting Makoto Nishimura, the local representative, the three of us McAlister, Doolin, and Ketchum knew the problem was more than a few radioactive cattle. We could see he feared the unknown.

Come with me, he said, escorting us to the exit of the airport terminal. We had flown into Fukushima from D.C., close to a year after the tsunami hit the power plant. Assembled by an NGO, when it heard of the problem, McAlister and Ketchum were found working on a dude ranch in Wyoming. Around the campfire we would glug down Maker's Mark and ice-cold bottles of Budweiser and sing half-forgotten verses of "The Old Chisholm Trail." Ketchum liked to rib McAlister, undermine his seriousness, repeating that his skin was dry as peppered jerky and stunk of mature elk carcass. McAlister didn't need words to reply. He would give us the finger or use his deerskin glove to whip-slap the soft part of our crowns. Doolin was dug up in Montana, east of Missoula. He was a thin, wiry man with a dark walrus moustache, reckoning he was a modern-day Johnny Ringo. He griped on the plane, for something like half the Pacific, about wanting a smoke and finding one of those hostess bars he had heard about.

Makoto Nishimura drove us in silence. He stared straight ahead, trying to avoid the carnage at the roadside. In the pale dawn light the landscape resembled a crude oil painting. The blacktop was cracked and chunks of asphalt were strewn across the land—like the craters on a lost moon. Limp tendrils of corkscrewed metal were gathered in piles, as if

13

ready for collection. Doolin offered him a cigarette. *Take one*, he said. *They're free.* Makoto Nishimura bowed his head slightly and carefully slipped one into his shirt pocket. Doolin grinned. *Come on, man. Light it up. Smoke it.* Makoto Nishimura politely ignored him and pointed out of the driver's-side window to a gyudon-ya restaurant.

We parked up. We stepped out of the car into the cloying humidity. We didn't have much of an idea of how things were being run. McAlister, who, always reading the same copy of the *Casper Star Tribune*, said the great wave had ravaged hundreds of houses and caused dogs and cats to disappear. We always listened to him, the glaze of his world-weary face adding gravity to his words. The building, he explained, was being used as the headquarters in dealing with lost pets. He tucked his newspaper under his arm, glanced at the brightening sun, licked his dry lips, and told us the officials were also responsible for dealing with the feral cows.

Makoto Nishimura coughed to get our attention. He was standing by the side of the building, one arm behind his back, the other angled toward the masonry. *Water came to here*, he said, running his fingers across the brick. Doolin snorted. People said what was really on their mind in his town. He thought Makoto Nishimura lacked emotion, that his stoic expression matched the blandness of his gray suit. Doolin turned away and slapped Ketchum's back as we entered the restaurant. The inside looked like an old fast food joint. We agreed the place was fancier than McDonald's, yet we kept feeling the property gave off a grim air. The dining area had been transformed into a low-grade operations center. The pink plastic tables and matching backstools had been shunted to the far side of the room, and a bank of computers and a large topological map had been installed in the middle. A dozen boxes containing animal photographs—names penned on the reverse—were circled in a loop, and a young woman was inspecting the pictures and checking the list pinned to her clipboard. Doolin was immediately all over her. He drooled over the cleanliness of her white cotton blouse and the tightness of her gunmetal-gray skirt. He traced his cigarette stub across one of the names on the list, pretending to understand kanji.

McAlister tugged Doolin's shirt and dragged him into the kitchen. Thick polyethylene sheets covered the floor, and the stainless steel surfaces reeked of bleach. We sized up the stack of pallid yellow radiation suits. Ketchum tossed off his Stetson and ran his hand through the remaining slicked wisps of his blond hair. He pawed at one suit and studied the laminated instructions tacked to the wall. He rolled his shoulders, as if to say we should get down to it. We stripped off our Wranglers and plaid shirts and worn buffalo leather boots and climbed into the suits. The masks slipped over our heads, creating a barrier between the outside world and us. Doolin smirked. *Goddamn hot in these things*, he said.

We were issued badges, which would turn a brilliant red if the radiation levels became fatal, and a Geiger counter that started clicking as soon as McAlister switched it on. He was worried. He had a kid back in Rawlins, and he needed to remain healthy to send half his paycheck to his ex-wife. In the last year, he had already suffered a herniated disc and a torn rotator cuff on the range. His savings were wiped out. Suzie was shacked up with some out-of-work cowhand, a guy who shotgunned tall cans of Rolling Rock and watched reruns of *Bonanza*. McAlister still loved her and, hell, hoped to win her back. We had all seen her picture, admired her full breasts and tight jean shorts, and fantasized of sleeping with her.

From a case of imported Winchester rifles, Makoto Nishimura passed out single-shot .22s. The sights were old, made of buckhorn iron, and were unlikely to accurately hit anything farther than thirty yards—though that didn't stop Doolin boasting he could split a woman's lip at any distance. He fingered the trigger and watched Makoto Nishimura circle an area on the map. *We go there*, he said. *Wagyu*. Doolin perked up when he saw his target and he sighted the rifle on the location and whispered *Boom!*

In the parking lot, Makoto Nishimura refused to wear a radiation suit, saying it was a mark of honor that he faced the city without protection. We argued with him, told him he was crazy, that his skin would crisp off in large translucent sheets. End up fried. Our words had little effect, and he waited patiently for us to stop the hectoring. Doolin slung his arm around him. He didn't understand the honor thing, but reckoned the Jap was brave. We switched vehicles. We needed something with more horsepower than the sedan. Makoto Nishimura led us to a beat-up Jeep coated in a powdery gray film. Doolin opened the driver's-side door, a touch of humility glossing his action, and asked him to lead the way.

15

We drove to the restricted area. Buzzed to get started. Ketchum sat in the front passenger-seat, rolled his window down halfway, reached around and drew a circle in the dirt. He was forming a plan of action. A way to find the cows. *You guys know anything about Wagyu?* he said. We knew a little, but not much. Ketchum explained the cattle were different from our steer: the meat was prized for its marbling and intense flavor—all due to the rugged uplands where they lived and the sake poured into the feed. *Tough sons of guns*, he added, and wound up his window.

As we crossed into Okuma Town, Makoto Nishimura spoke of the destruction, how his sister had been killed in the floods. Her bloated body lay undiscovered for six days. *Only by her teeth did we...* He seized up, and McAlister massaged his shoulder. We asked about her, trying to console him, but he didn't want to talk anymore. He switched on the radio and tuned it to blistering static. We became quiet, muscles tensed, as we considered the scenarios in which people had drowned. We imagined the greasy flesh and the cracked bones, the seawater pouring down spluttering throats. There was barely space in our minds to comprehend the glassy-eyed corpses floating in the wash. We replayed these visions of horror over and over until we saw the reactor on the horizon. A strange yellow haze masked the cooling towers and the plant took on the guise of a science fair diorama, squashed by a bad-tempered child. We weren't shocked. We disliked technology. Progress. Nature always won out. We could see this everywhere we looked. Gauzy heat waves rippled the air above the ocean and it appeared water and sky were joined, that we were in another world. It reminded us of the range, the widowed land we had left behind.

We zipped through the streets thinking about the feral cattle and then of the local herders who had gone to live with relatives. Doolin didn't care. He was an orphan and he often bragged about his foster parents being alcoholics, as if his upbringing were a badge of pride. Makoto Nishimura didn't stop once in the town, instead speeding onto a road that snaked into the hills and dead-ended at a wooden farmhouse topped with a thatched roof. On foot, we followed him, searching for dirt trails. Cow clues. Splatted on rocky outcrops we found desiccated scat. Doolin kicked a circle of the encrusted dung, frustrated by the lack of hoofmarks. In a low voice Makoto Nishimura said the Wagyu had become spirits, and he showed us the warehouse and talked again and again of the wizened men

16

and women withering away inside. The concrete building resembled a prison, the sharp angular walls cutting against the sky. None of us wanted to do any hard time in there. Doolin's six years inside reminded us of that. As we returned to the Jeep, Makoto Nishimura seemed different. Whether the change was related to his sister, we weren't sure. We talked about his radiation sickness—his mottled gray skin and rimmed yellow eyes—and asked him about his worsening condition. Makoto Nishimura said, *Good. Keep searching.*

In the east of the city we came across a large public park, and Ketchum speculated the cows grazed on the sprawls of long grass. We hiked past a dried-up pond and hooked around to a baseball field overgrown with knotweed. Ketchum stooped down and rubbed a single blade of grass between his gloved fingers, the plastic brightening with chlorophyll sheen. We trailed him to the pitcher's mound, where he found hoofmarks in the dust. He figured we could trap the cattle. Enclose them within a makeshift corral, using a roll of concertina wire. Near the park's entrance we cordoned off a section of the street, and hammered the barbs into the wall of a yakatori bar, finally unspooling a great curve of wire around an upended school bus. Doolin nailed the end to the doors of a pachinko parlor. He peered inside at the dozens of weird slot machines and grabbed a handful of steel balls from the floor and stared at the shiny spheres. *Odd country*, he said, and let them slip through his fingers. *They never heard of poker?* We joined back up with Makoto Nishimura, who was sitting in the Jeep. We explained our plan: a trail of corn feed to help funnel the beasts through the gap. He nodded and gave us the closest thing to a smile.

Just before nightfall, as we sat and waited in the dugout, we heard an ethereal braying from the grassy area behind the baseball field. We ran toward the noise. At least fifty cows, an amorphous group, were bumping into one another—colors changing from coal black to tan brown. As they fed on the corn feed, they plodded closer to the street. We circled around them, waiting for the right moment, smelling damp earth on their hides. Then McAlister fired a shot into the air. The herd charged, and we scattered. Ketchum and McAlister hid behind a large park map, while Doolin climbed on top of the school bus and sang out a *yeehaw!* The cattle thundered straight into the corral, haunches tearing against the barbs and spilling blood on the dirt. They turned, looking for an escape. Ketchum sprinted with the last coil of wire and nailed the end to a radiation placard, completing the fence. We hooted with laughter and patted each other on the back. Makoto Nishimura walked over from the dugout. Sweat beads formed on his gray brow. *The job is not yet done,* he said. Ketchum scrutinized him and realized he wanted us to shoot the cows. He pointed to our rifles and then to the skulls of the animals. *Shite kudasai,* he begged. *Please.* We studied the cattle and the deep sound of their breathing. Their eyes were bright and wet. McAlister slung his rifle at Makoto Nishimura's patent leather shoes. Ketchum and Doolin did the same. Makoto Nishimura shook his head and dropped to his knees, his face in his hands. McAlister inhaled a long breath and said, *Not what we signed up for.* We were sorry about his sister's death, about all the deaths, but more killing wasn't going to help. McAlister nodded for us to leave, and we jumped in the Jeep—Doolin grinning as he buckled up in the driver's seat. As we headed in the direction of the setting sun, we saw Makoto Nishimura pick up one of the rifles and enter the corral.

Flyer

In the months leading up to my ninth birthday, I bugged Father for a red wagon. He bought me one, of course—a Radio Flyer with a green bow tied around the handle. That morning I didn't wait to open my other presents. I just took the wagon onto the street and used it to move rocks from the neighbor's pond to a narrow culvert that separated the neighborhood from the beach. We lived in a large Catholic section of Coney Island, a ten-minute walk from Steeplechase Park. From my bedroom window, I could see the metal tower of the Parachute Jump ride and the people screaming as long steel ropes hoisted them up and down.

A few days after my birthday, I asked Father at breakfast if I could go to work with him. "Sure, Samuel," he said. "Just don't cause trouble, like last time." He ruffled my hair and smiled so widely I saw the toast still inside his mouth. He carried on reading the newspaper, and I toyed with the scrambled eggs on my plate and thought about the candy bar in my room. Father drank the rest of his coffee and said, "If you're finished, do the dishes." He left the table and soon after I heard him talking to my cousin, Pam, in their bedroom. I left my plate where it was and skipped to the front door. I peered through the glass panel at the neat piles of orange and brown leaves in the neighbor's garden and I felt an urge to kick the leaves, then bury them next to the pin oak that overlooked our house.

Pam called my name. I ignored her. "Samuel," she said again, this time louder. I turned to see Pam, hands on hips, her body inflated by a bubblegum-pink cardigan. She shook her head. Her brown hair framed her angular face like the women in her magazines, making her look older than she was. She hustled me to the hallway closet and made sure I put on my pencil-gray pea coat and thick woolen gloves.

Father kissed Pam on the cheek and whispered a gauzy goodbye into her ear. He had on mud-brown khakis and one of his old Navy shirts, the

19

epaulets unbuttoned and loose. He slung a cigarette in his mouth and grabbed my hand. At the door, he looked toward the bright sky and said a few words about the salt air. He was always talking about its benefits, as though breathing it in would cure any ailment. We took a short cut past the bathhouses so we could see the vast expanse of the ocean and Father could point out the smallness of the gulls. In the park, he ran a concession stand that sold ice-cream in the summer and popcorn and hot dogs in the fall. As we stepped onto the boardwalk, he explained that once a week a man came to check the stock levels. "He's important," he said. "Mr. Kendrick."

We entered the park through the workman's gate. Outside of a gray building, Father met some men I vaguely recognized. They talked about the end of the season and possible construction jobs in West Brighton. They shared cigarettes from a pack embossed with a camel and lit all four with one match. A grizzled older man with frothy-white hair mentioned it was time for work, and Father nodded and clapped his hands together. I followed him over to his concession stand, which was made of wood and painted a sharp green. The floor was a concrete slab covered in sawdust. The stand looked different from the last time I had seen it in the summer when bunting had been nailed to the frame and Fourth of July balloons were tied to the corner posts.

Father brushed past me to switch on the popcorn maker. He smoked while he poured kernels into the steel kettle. The cigarette hung on his lower lip, even as he used a stained rag to wipe the glass case. His taut arm muscles pulsed through his shirt, quite different from Pam's, which recently had become fat. He gave me a toothy smile and continued to work. All the while he mumbled words as if crossing items off a list. "Napkins. Soda," he said. After setting up a row of Coca-Cola bottles on a plank shelf, he picked me up and plopped me on the counter. His cheeks were red, and I noticed for the first time the creased skin near his eyes.

"Take this," he said, giving me one of the bottles.

"It's cold," I said, motioning that I was going to jump down.

"Stay where you are," he said.

I drank a few sips and watched him walk to the gray building about fifty feet away. I poured the rest of the Coke on the ground in front of the stand. I wondered how big the brown puddle would become. The liquid fizzed as it swirled over the gravel and expanded out to resemble a large burnt pancake. When Father carried back a cardboard box, he said it contained frozen hot dogs, and I hopped down and pressed my body against the popcorn maker to warm up. I squinted at the sun and wondered why the day was so cold. I asked Father about it and he told me to fetch a pail of water for the steam table.

* * *

In the afternoon, Father pointed out Mr. Kendrick. He was leaning against a faded sign that read PAVILION OF FUN and talking to a small group of men. Underneath his sports jacket he wore a white cotton shirt and a black leather belt, which divided his stick-thin body in half. He had a sunburned face, but I wasn't sure from where. He reminded me of the old people who visited the park from Florida and complained about the rain being cold and wet. Even when he came over to Father's stand, he walked as though he suffered from arthritis.

Mr. Kendrick grunted Father's name and opened a plain ledger that resembled a Bible. Every now and then he jotted a brief note on one of its pages. Sometimes he tutted when he found stock out of place or inventory missing. At the rear of the stand, he peered inside a large wooden crate and pointed his pencil at the things he was counting.

He glanced up at Father. "Your son been stealing?"

Father shook his head and continued to serve a middle-aged couple their hot dogs. "Lost five bags of kernels last week," he said. "Flood damage from the rain."

Mr. Kendrick nodded. "Hell of a storm," he said and scrawled a few words. He came over to me and settled his hand on my shoulder. He sported thick fingernails, clean and polished.

"Nice kid," he said, looking at Father. "Didn't mean any offense."

His grip tightened on my collarbone, and I went to hide behind Father. He was annoyed at my presence and he reached into his hip pocket.

"Take this," he said. "Don't tell Pam." He palmed me a quarter and told me to return in an hour.

I stored my pea coat under the gunnysacks behind the stand and ran toward the Parachute Jump, hoping to get a free ride like the one I enjoyed in the summer. When I saw the long line, I felt mad about having to wait. The feeling soon passed, and I bought a box of saltwater taffy and ate it as I explored the sideshows. For a while I lingered near the racetrack ride because I liked the stilted gallop of the mechanical horses.

Over by the frozen custard stand was a girl from my school. I didn't know her name, but I always thought she was pretty. She was barefoot and wore a candy-striped bathing suit with a dingy blue towel draped on her thin shoulders. She was shivering and she seemed lost. I shadowed her as she slipped through the crowds, ignoring the screams of other children enjoying the roller coasters and the Duck Hunt carnies offering the chance to win a prize. At the entrance to the Ferris wheel, she stopped and looked around. I imagined for a moment she had seen me watching her. But she stared in another direction and waved to a woman carrying a pair of red saddle shoes. The girl fastened the towel around her waist as a makeshift skirt and pulled back her blond hair and tied it with a rubber band. She reminded me of Pam and the way she did the same thing with her hair for Father.

I revisited the sideshows to win a gift for Pam. There was a game where you had to throw darts at playing cards tacked to a wall. To win a prize you had to reach a certain score. For a dime you got two darts. My first throw missed all the cards. I took my time for the second, making sure to sight the dart on the King of Spades. Before I threw the dart, I heard a voice from behind say: "Aim for the Nine of Hearts." I turned to see Mr. Kendrick, his thin body silhouetted against the bright sun.

"You need a score under ten to win," he said.

"Thanks," I said and threw the dart, its tip shaving the edge of the Nine.

"Too bad," he said, patting me on the back. "Does your father know you gamble?"

"Darts are fun."

He smirked. "What's your name?"

"Samuel."

He gestured toward my taffy. "Do you want another box?"

"No, thanks."

"I'm Mr. Kendrick," he said.

"I know."

He stared at my face, trying to work me out. The longer he inspected me, the more I felt embarrassed. I was sure he could feel the heat from my cheeks. He spoke to the man running the sideshow, and the man passed him a brown bear decorated with a crimson bow tie. He tried to give me the bear, but I refused to take the silly toy. I walked on, wondering what he would do next. I found it funny that he pursued me, the fat bear under his arm. The other side of the sideshow, by a row of filled trash baskets, he overtook me and we both stopped.

"Do you like the park?" he asked.

"Sometimes."

He placed two fingers under my chin and raised my head so our eyes met. "You look like a girl," he said.

"I'm not," I said, stepping back.

"You have girl lips."

"Maybe you're thinking of my cousin Pam. She has girl lips."

He laughed in a mean way, and I decided not to speak to him anymore. Then I wondered if I did have girl lips. And I touched them; Mr. Kendrick watching the whole time.

An icy wind blew through us, and I remembered my pea coat hidden behind Father's stand.

"It's cold," he said, smiling. "You should take my jacket."

"No, I'm all right."

He smiled again as a family strolled past. When they reached the sideshows, he took out a shiny metal flask and sank a long swig. He looked around and then offered it to me.

"This will warm you up," he said.

"I'm not thirsty."

"Just a sip." He held the flask close to my mouth.

"I already had a Coke."

"Come on. Try it."

"It smells bad."

He grinned. In a way, he was handsome. Different from Father: a little younger, his hair darker and well groomed. He hid the flask in his jacket pocket.

"Goodbye," I said.

23

"Where are you going?"

"The beach."

"Give me a second, I'll come with you."

I didn't wait for him. I sprinted so there was a reasonable distance between us. Weaving through the crowds, I headed toward the main gate. Now and again I let him catch up, but I always made sure he remained a dozen yards behind. "Slow down," he said several times. When he said this I ran faster, occasionally turning to watch him struggle, to see his legs tight and awkward.

Outside of the park, I started for the boardwalk. Men and women mingled by the attractions, pointing and laughing at the freak shows and the wax figure museum. They drank soda and ate hot peanuts and fresh doughnuts. The air smelled of strong cologne and cheap perfume. There were families retreating from the chill wind sweeping across the beach. A group of teenagers were holding out, wrapped in bed sheets and surrounded by empty bottles of Thunderbird.

As I ran onto the beach, sweat gathered on my brow. I was hot and the ocean looked tempting. Its surface had darkened to a deep blue. Mr. Kendrick stalked me across the dirt-yellow sand. He was not a fast runner and he must have been tired. Breathing hard, he held his side as if suffering with a stitch. I laughed; he was nothing like Father. At the water's edge, I stripped down to my underwear and flung my body, belly-first, into the cool water. In the distance I could see the gulls Father always talked about. They soared high in the air, serene and free, and I swam toward them. It was twenty yards before I glanced again at the shore. Mr. Kendrick had stopped short of the ocean. He waved the bear above his head.

"Can't you swim?" I shouted.

He narrowed his eyes as he studied the water and his face reddened a little as though he were embarrassed. His hair was damp and unkempt, and I saw the creamy untanned part of his scalp. With his heel he marked a spot in the sand, flung the bear aside, and took off his sports jacket. He appeared to catch a glimpse of the lifeguard tower far down the beach. Then he unzipped his pants and unbuttoned his white shirt, settling his clothes on top of his jacket. He paused before removing his shoes and socks. His body was thinner than I had first thought. He had jutting ribs and reedy muscle on his legs.

"Come back," he said. "I want to show you something."

"Jump in," I said.

He dipped his left foot in the shallows. He grimaced as he stepped forward. He waded through the water for as long as possible. Then he slid his upper torso in, trying not to submerge his head. He swam with short, flapping strokes that left a trail of white foam in his wake. As he got closer to me, he shouted, "Samuel!" I raced on, harder and faster than before. For thirty yards I practiced my front crawl and my breaststroke, ably dealing with the growing waves. I did the backstroke for a while. So I could see him struggling with the breakers.

"Over here," I called out to him.

"Slow down."

I threw a thick clump of kelp, stinking of brine, at Mr. Kendrick. It missed him, but caught the attention of the gulls circling overhead and they flew down to investigate, their long yellow beaks hitting the water first. The gulls angered Mr. Kendrick, and he swam toward me with greater determination. He grabbed my ankle, and I kicked out, hitting him square in the jaw.

"You shouldn't play so tough," he said.

I giggled at his silly words and this made him madder.

He continued to chase after me, the two of us getting farther from the shore. When I turned to get my bearing, I noticed Mr. Kendrick was fighting against the chill of the water. His limbs hardened, and his breaths got deeper. Glassy-eyed, a look of horror crossed his face as a large whitecap rolled his way. I laughed at him, and he stopped swimming to say something. He garbled a few words I couldn't quite hear. His head dipped under the water as the wave engulfed him. I watched his last location to see if he would reemerge. When he didn't surface, I was glad. He was gone and wouldn't talk about me with Father.

On the beach, I dressed quickly and ran home. By the time I reached my neighborhood, the sky was violet and the air left me frozen. My body shivered and my hands felt jittery. In the front garden, I leaned against the pin oak and neatened my hair and tied my shoelaces in loose bows. I crept around the house to the backdoor. Pam was singing in the kitchen, and I could smell tomato soup. I stole inside to see Father sitting at the table, drinking coffee and reading the newspaper.

Pam caught me by the collar. "Your father told you one hour. You were meant to come right back."

"What's the time?"

Pam shook her head. "Why are you wet?" she said.

"Swimming," I replied.

"It's forty degrees outside," Father said, closing the sports section. He rose from his chair and reached inside his jacket for his cigarettes. "I told you not to cause trouble." He rolled one cigarette between his fingers, laid it flat on the table, and exited the kitchen. I heard the front door open and slam close.

I glanced down the hallway to my bedroom.

"Stay there," said Pam. She went to the storage closet and returned with a fresh baby blue towel. She rubbed me down, muttering the whole time about my skin being ice-cold. She wrapped the towel around my shoulders and fixed me a bowl of soup.

Later in the evening, the neighbor came to see Father. They talked for a short while in the living room. From my bed I tried to eavesdrop on their conversation. I heard my name mentioned several times and then heavy footsteps. Father entered my room, his face wan and gray, and delivered a set of instructions. "You must make amends," he said finally. Before lights out, I pulled my wagon to the culvert and moved the rocks back to the neighbor's pond.

The Lake

Ruth held up a large roadmap of Kansas against the passenger-side window. Bright sunlight bled through the thin paper, washing out the towns, blending together the endless miles of farmland. "I think we're here," she said, pointing to a red line in the middle. She seemed annoyed that I had glanced over and hadn't said anything. We were driving to a lake I visited as a boy. I didn't care much, but Ruth insisted on us taking a vacation, going somewhere different and away from the noise and dirt of the city. This was my first time back in Kansas since I moved across the country for graduate school in the late eighties. She had never been out this far west, living the last few years on the Upper East Side.

"Where do you think we are, Jim?" Ruth asked. She kept one hand on the map and rested the other on my leg. She gently squeezed the fleshy piece of muscle above my knee. It was a kind, almost unconscious gesture—one she rarely did these days. "Do you recognize anything?" Her voice trailed off as though she were distracted by something she had seen. The fields of corn and wheat had been the same for the last hour, only punctuated by the odd cottonwood and sun-bleached farmstead.

I said, "Only why I left."

Ruth emitted a sharp laugh and took back her hand. She folded the map and placed it in the glove compartment. Her actions were always graceful and measured. Even the way she coughed or sneezed was nothing but light, delicate motions that came and went in an instant.

"Sometimes, it's good to come home," she said.

I nodded even though I hadn't meant to. I tried to hide my agreement by looking down at her legs. She wore a radiant yellow sundress with tight elastic straps that revealed the slight curve of her flat chest. The freckles that ran from her shoulders to her back reminded me of how beautiful she was when we first met—then both of us divorcees of several years—and even beyond to her previous husband, of whom I had seen pictures: a young couple sunbathing on a New England beach.

"Focus on the road," she said.

"I know where we are."

For a short while we both stared ahead, unwilling to face each other. I thought about the long drive that had taken hours through Pennsylvania, and left short bathroom breaks and half-smoked cigarettes in Columbus and St. Louis, and later a night in a colonial-style hotel in Kansas City. We had talked for part of the way; mostly chitchat about mortgage payments and upcoming dinners with several of her friends. At one point she commented on the beauty of a brick cottage off in the distance, and I responded with an observation about the miles that lay ahead.

"Maybe the radio will help," she said, turning it on. "A local station or something." She fiddled with the dial, finding only static and the faded words of a preacher. Now and again we could hear terse evocations of sin and guilt. She played with her wedding ring, rotating it around and around. In front, the road rose as we neared a low range of green hills dotted with buckthorn. Warm air rolled over the prairie grass and the static grew louder on the radio.

"Switch it off," I said. "There's a gas station up ahead. We can ask there."

The place was a one-pump station with a small grocery store-cum-diner on the concrete forecourt. A man close to my father's age filled the tank and pointed to the diner's side entrance. Inside, I ate a greasy hamburger and drank a thick chocolate malt. Ruth refused to eat and sat in silence, nursing a cup of herbal tea. We watched the occasional traffic instead of talking. A rusted Buick sedan passed, then a mud-splattered tractor, and a panel truck advertising BRIAN'S LOCK & KEY. After I finished eating, I bought a cheap six-pack of ice-cold beer. The clerk, who could have been the attendant's son, told me the lake was thirty miles down the road. "No signs until you're there," he said.

Back in the car I gunned the engine. I planned to approach the lake by the dam that bordered its southern edge, show her the strange rectangular shape and talk about the lake really being a reservoir, an early remnant of the homesteaders who settled here a century before. Somehow, though, we ended up at the northern end where broad, leafy elm and straggly creosote bushes blocked our view of the water. The road curved in great sweeps, giving us hints of our destination. Farther on we passed a young couple hiking and an unmanned ranger's station. A quarter-mile past the station, the tree line opened up and I parked on a grassy area that overlooked the brass-colored water. The sun was close to the horizon, flooding the clouds with brilliant oranges and reds. The view was similar to my childhood memories of long, dusty summers camping near the shore. Days were spent swimming and fishing, and walking around the lake and the hills. Years later my parents never forgave me for leaving Kansas, for not settling down and taking over the farm.

Ruth stretched her arms and made a pleased moaning sound. She unpinned her hair, letting it fall on her shoulders, and she played with the ends. It was dyed dishwater blond and the roots were gray and brittle. I passed her a beer and grabbed one for myself. I was surprised she accepted the beer so easily. She rarely drank, as she claimed alcohol was the reason for her first marriage's demise.

"I feel sixteen," she said. "Like this is a date."

"I wish it was. I never went on that many."

We drank one beer apiece and then each started another. Ruth slid her tongue inside the lip of the bottle and gulped down the fizzy brown liquid. She had said in the past she used this technique to prevent her lipstick from smudging. She hadn't worn lipstick, though, for the last few months. Watching the sunset we became warm and comfortable on the cream padded leather seats. The dashboard clock read just after seven o'clock and my beer was tepid and had gone flat. I drank it anyway.

After a while I noticed Ruth studying me. Her eyes were slightly glazed and her mouth was open, expectant. Then she started to laugh; a strange sailing laugh that I had never heard from her.

"What's so funny?"

"Nothing," she said, still laughing a little.

"Come on. What is it?"

"Never mind," she said. "You wouldn't understand."

"Try me."

She crossed her legs toward me and finished the remains of her second beer. "I just imagined you as a boy. All red cheeks and full of energy."

"You're drunk," I said and kissed her on the temple. The lines on her face were clearer now and her crow's-feet pinched together as she concentrated on a flock of Canadian geese landing on the water.

"I'm glad we came," she said, facing me. "Perhaps we could stay with your parents?"

"That won't work," I said. "They live hours from here."

She balanced her beer on the dashboard and ran her hands through her hair, tucking several loose strands behind her ears. "You don't talk about them much."

"How about a motel? There's one in town."

"Do you miss them?"

"We could sleep here." I gestured toward the backseat.

"I'm too old to be sleeping in cars."

"No, you're not."

"I am. You are, too."

I flipped the sun visor down and examined my face in the mirror. My complexion was wan and gray and matched my salt-and-pepper hair, which was thinning on top. The only dash of color came from my short-sleeved Hawaiian shirt. The shirttails were tucked tightly into my khaki shorts, revealing the bulge of my stomach. I looked ridiculous, like a middle-aged man trying to recapture his twenties.

"Sorry," she said.

"It's all right."

"So, what town do they live in?" she said.

"I told you. It's far from here."

"I know *you* told me."

From past experience I could count on Ruth not letting the subject drop. "They live on a small farm. Near Beloit."

She made a pretense of gratitude, raising her arms as if to say *thank you.*

"How about a walk before it gets too dark?"

"I'm tired," she said.

I took my cigarettes out and wound the window all the way down.

"Will you smoke outside?"

"We are outside. This is the great land you wanted to see."

Ruth's shoulders tightened and she arched her back as though she wanted to curl up into a ball. She didn't say anything, and I thought about the state of our relationship, how it was careening to an end, and how this trip had been a last chance for redemption. We had known each other for five years, married less than two. Now it seemed like we had married out of convenience, that we were in search of companionship, not love.

"I'm going to have a look around," I said, after a minute.

"Do what you want," she said.

I unbuckled my seatbelt and removed the key from the ignition.

"Leave the keys," she said.

"What for?"

"I might need them."

I opened the door. "Don't do anything stupid," I said, placing the keys on the center console.

Ruth's lips turned down and her eyes narrowed. "Close the door," she said, cranking her seat into the recumbent position.

I tapped the roof and set off, following a dirt path down to the shore. Upon reaching an embankment covered in parched yellow grass, I glanced back at the car. It was parked at an odd angle, the hood a quarter-turn away from the lake. I could barely make Ruth out; just a dark, flat shadow slumped in the passenger seat, perhaps already sleeping. I was glad she had stayed behind and I thought about a future without her.

At the water's edge, I shielded my eyes to study the shimmering waves lapping the shore. There was a thin band of shingle that stretched for miles around the lake. I inhaled a long drag on my cigarette and blew the smoke toward the sky, and I listened to the gentle rhythmic pulse of the waves. The loamy smell of the silt was calming, and I flicked the cigarette into the water. The sky was turning a pale violet and hawks flew over the dam in the distance. Its large concrete wall served as a barrier, protecting the small college town on the other side. Invigorated by the beer and a sense of freedom, I started at a fast pace for the dam. Less than a hundred yards down the shore, I stopped to get my breath. My forehead was damp with sweat. I sat for a moment and remembered how Ruth talked me into this trip, and how I could not fathom why I had agreed.

I slipped off my navy blue canvas shoes and paced barefoot across the gray and brown rocks. Past an outcrop of green ferns was a boy staring intently at a teardrop boulder. He appeared to be twelve or thirteen and wore flannel shorts and a red T-shirt stenciled with a faded picture of some rock band I didn't recognize. His left wrist and palm were wrapped in fresh white gauze, and he struggled with his healthy hand to lift a good-sized rock.

"What are you doing?" I said.

He pointed to the boulder, which I could now see was an upturned seal. The mound of pale gray flesh was supine. One fin was angled skyward and looked malformed or eaten away by parasites.

"Checking it's dead," he replied, his gaze fixated on the seal.

I circled the body. The seal's face was squashed hard against the ground. Its eyes were vacant and black—held steady by pouches of fat. "It's dead," I said. I could smell rancid flesh and the glutinous blubber putre-fying from the inside out.

"Where did it come from?" he asked.

"Not sure." I knew there were no natural lakes in Kansas and besides that most seals lived in the sea.

"Maybe it escaped from the zoo," he said.

"Maybe." It occurred to me that the seal had traveled from the Great Lakes and swum up the river that fed the reservoir, or that the seal had been dumped here as a fraternity prank. While I considered these ideas, the boy tried with both hands to pick up the rock. He winced and dropped it, muttering something under his breath.

"What happened to your arm?" I said.

"I fell over."

"Playing a game?"

"No, just fell over." He rubbed his injured wrist, leaving dirt on the gauze. "I don't like the lake. There's nothing to do."

"I used to swim and fish here."

"I don't want to do that."

"Yeah, me neither."

"I don't want to end up like this thing." He offered a weary look to the seal.

"You're a smart kid," I said. "Where are your parents?"

He pointed over his shoulder. Half a mile or so down the shore was a bullet-gray RV and an orange dome tent. I watched the campsite, wondering if his mother or father would make an appearance. I pulled the cigarettes out of my shirt pocket and put one in my mouth.

"You shouldn't smoke," the boy said.

"I know."

"Can I have one?" He gave me a goofy grin.

Before I could answer, I heard a distant shout. Through the ferns, I spied a man around my own age standing on the steps of the RV.

"Your father?" I said.

The boy nodded. "He wants me to go back," he said and picked up a palm-sized rock. He weighed the rock in his hand then threw it at the seal's belly. I expected it to go right through, to reveal the insides of the creature. The rock just bounced off, the seal's skin undulating for what felt like minutes. The boy made a face as if to say *your turn*, and I bent down to pick up a rock of my own. We heard again the man call out. It was a deep guttural sound that could have been the boy's name, that could have been mine. The boy threw another rock, hitting the seal in the face. Its snout bloodied and one eye leaked a clear liquid. In the distance, the man checked the tent and then rubbed his brow. A woman joined him and the two walked to the shore and stared at the graying water. I faced the boy and placed my hand on his shoulder. I told him not to worry and the two of us stood above the seal, throwing rocks at its battered torso until it became too dark.

33

Diminuendo

Driving with one hand on the steering wheel, Phillip Kavanagh placed the other on the radio dial, tuning the radio to WNIB. The speakers spat out static, and Phillip blamed the neighborhood kids who had broken his aerial the day before. He knew they saw him as a loner, the weirdo who lived on the block. He reassured himself he didn't care as he left Chicago and took the back roads, relying on his knowledge of the state to zip through the dark terrain—a land sometimes lit by a neon sign for a truck stop or a spotlight on another WELCOME TO. He smirked when he read the town names and the small population numbers. Even when he made quick stops in Pontiac for gas and Mt. Vernon for coffee, he could not wait to continue. By dawn he saw the sign for Clarksville—a town he thought was south of Randolph—and he re-checked the address written on the reverse of his contact's business card. Milo had told him the house of Oskar Vesely, the once-famous Czech violinist, would be easy to find. Phillip pulled over his aging Buick sedan and studied the road ahead. The asphalt glistened from the early morning dew and cut through fields of corn, ending somewhere in the flattened green hills.

There was something unnerving about the farmland, he felt, something about the Stradivarius that awaited him being in such a cultureless area. Most of his career he bought and sold modern reproductions and the occasional late-model Amati. This 1698 Stradivarius was known as the "Baron Knoop," one of eleven Stradivari violins once owned by the collector Baron Johann Knoop, a man of mixed Russian and German stock, who helped run his father's vast empire of cotton mills.

A mile up the road, Phillip stopped at a two-pump gas station to buy a packet of cigarettes. The attendant was a burly man who wore a feed-store cap with the brim pulled low. He gave Phillip directions and told him the two towns were in fact one community, divided by a dried-up river,

35

and the place he was looking for was on the outskirts of Randolph. Phillip gunned the engine and drove in the direction the attendant had advised. A single-lane road led him into the countryside and eventually to a large house painted white and bordering a fallow field and a small thicket. After parking in the gravel drive, near to the sagging front porch, he studied the pleated shades pulled down throughout the first floor. He rolled down his window to take a closer look. The place appeared deserted, or at least temporarily abandoned, and he eyed the house number to confirm it was the right address. He watched for any sign of movement. A lone whip-poor-will called somewhere in the distance, although he could not place where.

He exited the car and walked across a narrow streak of flagstones. He knocked on the door and straightened his necktie as he waited. A thin, underweight woman with curled hair opened the door. She was of a similar age to him—her late fifties—but she had youthful eyes and wore a cream satin dress and a pearl rope necklace. Her arms were crossed tightly and her face had an expression of fright as though she knew Phillip, yet did not want to see him. He attributed this, he realized, to her complexion scrubbed clean, not a sign of makeup, and he imagined how the woman would look if she wore mascara or scarlet lipstick.

"Is Mr. Vesely home?"

"I'm sorry," she said, her tone flat and hard. "No visitors today."

"I'm here about the violin."

"Mr. Kavanagh?"

"Yes," he said, fishing out a business card from his wallet and presenting it to her as if it were an exotic gift.

She studied his name for a moment and then allowed him into the hallway. She led him to an anteroom and instructed him to wait. She walked through a pair of white French doors, turned to the left, and disappeared from his view. Phillip paced up and down. His soles clacked on the varnished floor and drew attention to his nervousness. He had waited his whole life to hold a violin like the Baron Knoop, an instrument that had only been touched by a handful of people. He refocused his thoughts on the framed photograph displayed on the marble plinth in the corner. The sepia-toned picture was decades old. Standing in front of the Tonhalle in Zurich was a young girl, who he assumed was the woman, and

36

a dour-faced man easily recognizable as Oskar Vesely.

The woman reentered the anteroom and crossed her arms. "I'm afraid my father can't see you."

"The appointment was arranged."

"I'm sorry. Things will be better tomorrow."

"It won't take long."

"No," she said, scratching the fleshy part of her palm. Half-smiling, she appeared to want to backtrack on her tone and compensate for her words. "I don't want him to be disturbed." She glanced over her shoulder as though she had heard a sound.

"Is everything all right?"

"Yes," she said. "But you have to leave."

As she closed the door, he was not sure what to make of this turn of events. He knew Oskar Vesely was old, somewhere in his eighties, and probably suffered from the diseases of old age. Phillip's own father had died from the repercussions of senile dementia and he remembered the pain of those last months in the hospital, his father asking for a cold glass of water over and over, and how, when he finally refused, his father said he was a lousy doctor.

Phillip drove into town and checked into a sixty-dollar-a-night motel. The long two-story strip had faded pastel walls and a shared concrete balcony that overlooked a large parking lot. He lugged his brown leather suitcase inside and inspected his room, finding a twin bed with blue-frilled sheets. He placed his case next to the nightstand and glared at the television set bolted into a monstrous steel stand. When he noticed the amateurish watercolor above the headboard, he grabbed the pine frame and flipped it around. In the bathroom, he splashed cold water onto his face and stroked his chin as he considered shaving. Flinty gray hairs dotted his five-o'clock shadow, and he searched his case for his razor. "Damn it," he said, finding it missing. He slammed the case shut, his mind returning to his father. Before seeing Oskar, it had been many months since he had thought of the hospital. In the time after his father's passing he had tried to grieve by visiting the grave, but he felt a crippling hollowness on every drive to the cemetery. For six months, he regularly saw a therapist to talk things through. The sessions had not worked—only throwing himself into discovering rarer and rarer violins had some effect.

Milo's locating of the Baron Knoop had struck Phillip as cathartic. But here in the hotel room his emotional progress had fallen away, grudgingly replaced by the last memories of his father's death.

To clear his head, he decided to take a walk downtown. He passed an Art Deco theater undergoing renovation. Two men in beige coveralls were bolting the words CLASSIC FILMS to the front of the marquee. A light drizzle began to fall, and Phillip scanned the stores to find a place to wait out the shower. He entered a gift shop as the rain pelted against the window and distorted his view of the men dashing for cover. Browsing the aisles he found English-style teapots, white doilies, and buttercup-yellow fondue sets. On the shelf of the back wall was a cheap pine violin. He looked to the storeowner—a woman in a pilled winter sweater and busy with a middle-aged couple selecting tablecloths—and picked the violin and bow up. He blew dust out of the F-holes and wedged the violin between his chin and neck. The cold chinrest felt familiar and reassuring and he rested the bow on the strings, inhaled a deep breath, and eked out a few notes. Softly he drifted into playing Paganini's "Caprice No. 13," trying to find the finesse he once displayed. He stopped a minute into the piece. The sound was coarse, grating to his tuned ear.

"You're good," said the owner.

"No," said Phillip, startled. "Not really."

"You played as the heavens came down."

He tried to give the violin to the woman.

"It was wonderful! Truly wonderful. Are you sure I can't persuade you?" she said. "I picture you enjoying this."

He considered her question then returned the violin. "It needs to go to a better home."

Farther down the street, Phillip purchased a razor and a toothbrush and a tube of toothpaste from a drugstore on the corner. The cashier told him this was the first real rain for a month. "Thank God," she added, "my yard looks like the Dust Bowl." He asked her about a decent place to get a coffee, and she told him JOE'S a block over was all right.

At the diner, he ate steak and eggs and drank several cups of black coffee as he deliberated his chances of assessing the violin the next day. He worked on commission, finding rare violins, occasionally cellos as well, and evaluating them for auction. In his line of work, one or two sales a week were enough to keep his modest greystone in Logan Square and to attend concerts and recitals at Orchestra Hall. He had been a keen violinist in his younger days, even deemed *brilliant*. But still part of the rank-and-file—never first chair. At one point, when he lived in Cleveland, he had envisaged a life working in a Midwest orchestra, performing the standard repertoire. An endless repeat of Mozart, Tchaikovsky, and Beethoven, he felt, would have eviscerated his love of music. His habit of collecting sheet music, blitzing the parchment with his pencil annotations, expanded his interests into the esoteric, the obscure, the neglected, and he discovered Goldmark's *Violin Concerto*, Shostakovich's *Symphony No. 15*, the romantic orchestral work of Gottschalk, and Rochberg's *Slow Fires of Autumn.*

On the way back to the motel, ahead of him, he saw the flat concrete bridge that joined the two towns. He considered exploring the dried riverbed and seeing if he could discover the cause, but he thought better of it and retreated to his room. There, he hung his suit over the air-conditioning unit bolted beneath the window in the hope the chilled air would keep it fresh. He called Milo and left a message on his answering machine, asking his advice on how to deal with Oskar Vesely. He perched on the foot of the bed. The cheap linen reminded him of the last vacation he took with his ex-wife, Vanessa, a five-day break to a health spa in central Ohio. They spent most of the time apart; she splurged on full-body massages and tennis lessons with the club pro, while he took long strolls in the wooded grounds. By the time they returned to Cleveland, it was clear to him the marriage was over. He carried this memory into the shower, and it bugged him, even later when he switched on the television and smoked a cigarette.

* * *

Phillip had tried other jobs after he had ended his performing career. He offered private violin lessons to high schoolers, instructing them in the finer points of bowing and finger positioning, but stopped when the teenagers' lack of talent or poor work ethic disheartened him. Vanessa, who worked in medical billing, found him a filing clerk position at her company. He lasted a month before he accepted a new job at a regional production company, scoring commercial music for radio and television. A dozen years later he quit that job, too, and the relationship, and started his own business. Now he was knocking on Oskar Vesely's door, which—until recently—seemed quite unimaginable. In all earnestness he hoped he would see the woman again. Her slack pale skin and pointed nose reminded him so much of his ex-wife that he found it uncanny and in a sense attractive. The woman carried herself with a sensual air, quite unconsciously, and he wondered if she were married or if she had paid any attention to him the day before. He was unsure. Reaching for his necktie, he touched only starched shirt. His tie, he remembered, was on the nightstand—looped and knotted with a Windsor. Embarrassed as the woman opened the door, he rubbed the nub of heavy jowl under his chin. Her eyes widened as she recognized him.

"Good morning," he said.

"Come in," she said. "Mr. Lorenz advised us you would return."

Phillip nodded, mystified as to why Milo had called here and not his motel. He followed her down the hallway—past the oil landscapes and framed newspaper reviews of Oskar Vesely's performances. There was also a large family portrait picturing Oskar's five children and a dozen grandchildren. He knew a great deal about Oskar's career: his work with the New York Philharmonic, his later years with the Boston Symphony Orchestra, and his famed solo recordings of Bach's sonatas and partitas. He also learned a long time ago that Oskar married four times. His first wife had died in the pogroms after the Nazi annexation of Czechoslovakia. Oskar fled the country with an uncle and had settled in a studio apartment on the Lower East Side and taught at Julliard until the war ended. This story was well known—the subsequent relationships were more opaque, mired, as they were, in rumored infidelity and domestic violence.

Instinctively, Phillip caught up to the woman so that they walked side by side. "Are you Karolina?"

"No, that's my half-sister."

"I'm sorry."

"Anna." She turned to him and looked coolly into his eyes. "Now my father is hard of hearing. He has been for many years. So you will have to speak clearly and loudly."

"Of course."

They went into the large drawing room, which contained several sturdy bookcases, a teak sideboard that ran half the length of one wall, and a solid marble fireplace. Oskar was sitting close to the stone hearth, in a stately leather chair, with a book open in his lap. On the side table next to him was a brass reading lamp angled toward the pages. He wore a gabardine suit and sported a froth of wispy gray hair that diverted attention away from the brown liver spots on his forehead. Phillip, though, was drawn to the dark violin case behind the lamp. He felt light-headed in the presence of the Baron Knoop.

"Father, this is Mr. Kavanagh."

Glancing up for the first time, Oskar cleared his throat into his fist and looked at Phillip over the rim of his half-moon glasses, his rheumy eyes probing for meaning. Anna stood next to Oskar, stooped down so their faces were level, and spoke softly into his ear: "He's from the auction house."

Phillip stepped forward, wanting to clear up the misconception. "Not quite," he said. "I'm an independent evaluator. I work with Staunton's from time to time."

"Leave us," said Oskar to his daughter.

"Father..."

For a second the two were stalemated. The tension reminded Phillip of his wife and their arguments, their incompatibility.

"Find something else to do," he said, waving her away. His cheeks reddened and he flipped through the pages of his book.

Straightening up, Anna sighed. She opened her mouth as if to argue back, but no words came out—just the soft edge of a sad breath. "I'm sorry," she said, and left the room.

"I'm not sure what that was about, but I am very honored to—"

Oskar glanced over, his expression one of surprise that Phillip was still there. "Are you a religious man?" he said.

"Intermittently," replied Phillip, unsure how best to answer the question.

Emitting a croaky laugh, Oskar clapped his hands together.

"Can I ask what you are reading? Is it the Bible?"

Oskar appeared thrown by the question, as if he had not quite heard Phillip's words. He lifted up the book, which Phillip could now see was

41

Moby-Dick. "I wanted to read it one last time," he said, easing the novel back to his lap.

"I wish I had the time to read more."

Pinching the glasses off the bridge of his nose, Oskar held them at a distance, trying to examine Phillip in a new way. "Staunton's," he said. "That's on Main, near the theater."

"Chicago. Wicker Park, to be precise."

The place names seemed to reverberate within Oskar's mind and he repeated "Chicago" in a soft voice. He added, "I performed there on several occasions."

"Yes, in the seventies."

"Dangerous place," said Oskar, replacing his glasses. "One of the worse I've been to."

"Things are better now," said Phillip, watching Oskar dog-ear his page and close the book. He drummed his fingertips gently on the cover, and Phillip tried to figure out the pattern of the beats.

"I gather."

Phillip was impressed by Oskar's level of English. There was only a hint of an accent, as if Oskar's upbringing were a faint memory. He recalled a controversial statement Oskar had made in a magazine interview—was it six years ago?—about the Czech Republic, that the new country was not worth visiting. The remark, he remembered, was uttered shortly after Oskar's retirement. His final shows had been criticized for the less-than-perfect performances and in particular the critics had derided the deterioration of his playing. Phillip was not sure how the two incidents were connected, but he suspected Oskar's comments were the last blast of his spotlighted ego.

"Sadly," said Phillip, "I wasn't able to see you in concert. I was working in Cleveland."

Oskar touched the violin case, stroking the surface. His hands were ridged with blue veins, though the ones on his left were scabbed. "There comes a time in every man's life when he must part with that which he loves," he said. "But that time is not now."

"I don't understand."

"I apologize for wasting your afternoon, Mr..."

"Kavanagh."

"Yes, Kavanagh. Give my regards to Mr. Lorenz." He returned to his reading of *Moby-Dick*, his finger tracing the lines.

Phillip considered sitting down in an attempt to regain Oskar's attention, and he hovered by the chair for a few seconds, before changing his mind and leaving the room. On the way out, he saw Anna by the telephone stand, pretending to search through the directory. Her lips were pursed, and when he reached her, she attempted a weak smile.

"Is everything all right?" she asked.

"He doesn't want to sell it."

"I was afraid he might say that."

"He didn't even take the violin out of the case."

"My father is a difficult man, as you saw. The thing is he can't bear to touch it. In case it is his last opportunity to play."

"That may be true, but I have a business to run."

"I understand. I will talk to him."

Back at the motel, Phillip informed the manager he would be staying another night. He decided to buy a new suit. Something stylish that would impress Anna and mask the growing bulge of his potbelly. It had been many years since he last purchased a suit. He had felt little need post-marriage. If he managed to bring the Baron Knoop to auction, it would be the biggest sale of his twenty-year career. A modest estimate placed the violin at five-million dollars, and his five percent commission equaled a quarter of a million. His job was to appraise the workmanship, check to see if the violin was damaged in any way, and further to authenticate the provenance. To be sure it was a genuine Stradivarius and not a later copy or fake. On Main Street, he located a tailor who could alter an off-the-rack three-piece suit to fit Phillip's slightly disproportionate body. His legs and arms were gangly, which often meant his thin bony wrists stuck out an inch too far. The tailor measured Phillip, said the suit needed only minor adjustments, and would be delivered to the motel in the evening.

* * *

By the time Phillip arrived at Oskar Vesely's house, the rain had morphed into a downpour—easily dropping an inch on the parched lawn. He watched the wipers clear the windscreen, the motion spiking a

43

fascination with the temporary quarter-circles. Although he was concerned with what lay in the house, here he enjoyed a Zen appreciation for the simple *rat-a-tat* noise of the rain. It was only when he noticed the car was running low on gas that he thought of dashing for the front door. He stepped out, dodged a gathering puddle, and strode up the path cursing the weather and his lack of foresight in not bringing an umbrella. As he reached the porch, Anna opened the door. There was a slight puffiness beneath her eyes.

"Sorry about the weather," she said, letting him past. "It's been a strange year." She went to the closet and removed a towel. She handed it to Phillip, who proceeded to pat dry his face and then his suit and shoes.

"Thank you," he said, returning the towel. "That was most kind."

"Flashy suit," she observed, directing him down the hallway. "Did your wife pick it out?"

Phillip grinned. Although he felt a little foolish about that part of his life, he was flattered that she discovered his effort. The jacket, he found, was a reasonable fit—but the pants cinched his waist. "No, this was all me. It's been a long time since my ex-wife has warranted a say over my clothes."

"I'm sorry," she said, embarrassed. "It was rude of me to pry."

"Don't worry about it—we divorced eons ago. I bought the suit in town. Merriman's. Do you know it?"

"Yes, vaguely. I've not been in the store."

Anna peered through the top pane of the French doors and rapped sharply. The drawing room was blighted by stale, smoky air from the fire. Oskar appeared to be asleep in his chair, and Phillip went to the fireplace and rubbed his hands together to warm them. Large yellow flames flickered in the blackened arrangement of tipi logs, and, breathing in the cloying air, he wondered how long it had been since the windows were last cracked. Anna gently squeezed Oskar's palm. His eyes opened and he glimpsed Anna and then Phillip. Mindful of their last meeting, Phillip sat in the armchair opposite Oskar and attempted to maintain eye contact.

"I don't need a towel," said Oskar, his voice more alert than Phillip would have supposed.

"It's not for you, Father."

"Then take it away," he said, shaking his head.

"Mr. Kavanagh is here."

"Then brew the tea."

Phillip drew his shoulders together and leaned forward, trying to get a read on Oskar. He is enjoying these delays, he sensed. "I realize time is short and I would like to—"

"I'm eighty-one," he said.

Phillip was puzzled. "I'm not sure what you mean."

"I'm eighty-one-years-old," Oskar explained. "Tea is one of life's pleasures. Time should always be made for it."

"Yes, very well," he replied. He nodded at Anna. "I will have a cup."

"We have Assam and Ceylon," she said.

"Either is fine. Whichever you are drinking."

Anna mouthed an inaudible *yes*, and she headed to the recessed archway in the far corner.

Moby-Dick was on the table next to the violin case. If this was a game, Phillip thought, he would play it with small talk. "I see you're still reading Melville."

"I fear I always will be." Oskar raised the book, spun it around, and fingered the page number. "I had forgotten how long and digressive it is. The last time I read it I was on tour in Europe. The late eighties, I think."

"A strange period," noted Phillip, "what with the Cold War and—"

"All I remember are the long journeys through pure civilization. Trains. Such splendid trains. This book lasted me until Zurich."

Anna returned to the drawing room with a silver tray. Atop it were a china teapot with a blue-and-white garden design, two matching cups and saucers, and a plate of kolache. The crusts of the round pastries were golden brown and the fat centers were filled with generous dollops of bright red fruit.

"Anna was with me. It was our first trip with just the two of us. Do you recall that European tour?"

"I don't think you finished your book."

"Perhaps you're right," said Oskar, spying the baked treats. "What are those?"

"Strawberry," said Anna. "Your favorite." She placed the tray on the sideboard and poured the tea and then set aside the kolache on small, square plates. Her movements, as she brought Phillip and Oskar a cup and a plate each, were graceful as though she had once trained as a ballerina.

Oskar refused to take his drink. "I don't want tea."

Anna was still for a moment. "Are you sure, Father?"

"Yes," he said, glaring at the kolache.

"Are you joining us?" asked Phillip, trying to break the tension.

"This is a business matter," barked Oskar. "Anna is not important."

Phillip was shaken by Oskar's statement. He could not figure out the nature of their relationship. He wanted to say a few words to bolster Anna's side but he felt constrained by his position. Virtuosos, he knew from experience, were often temperamental and self-obsessed. He wondered if there was another reason, a connection to Oskar's cognitive degeneration. His father had acted similarly, berating him for bringing the wrong colored grapes or switching the TV channel away from The *Price Is Right* or *Jeopardy!*

Anna snatched her father's plate. "Excuse me," she said. She swept out of the room without closing the French doors behind her.

Without another word, Oskar opened the case and lifted out the silk bag that protected the Baron Knoop from being scratched. He slid the violin out and held it firmly in both hands. The maple construction was coated in a rich, walnut oil varnish. Phillip was aware of the idea that this added volume to the sound and produced an exquisite resonance. Though this was hard to prove, he liked to believe in the magical craftsmanship of Antonio Stradivari. Thinking back, he had heard the difference in Oskar's recording of Pisendel's concertos, the brilliance of three men's achievements coalescing in fine unison, and he wished he could again listen to the concertos, to have Oskar pick out his favorite sections.

Oskar held the violin under his chin and stared down the strings.

"May I hear you play?"

"No," said Oskar. "That would not be wise." His face turned to disgust, as if such an act were an abomination. Shoring the violin in his lap, he eyeballed Phillip. "I would like the violin in the hands of a deserving man, a young musician who could benefit the most."

"Of course." He balanced the plate on his knee and waited for Oskar to relinquish the Baron Knoop.

"It takes years to appreciate the sound," Oskar reiterated. "To hear the nuance of the note."

"Is price important?"

"I am merely a caretaker," he said, shifting in his chair. "The Baron Knoop has been looked after by better men than me."

"Surely not."

Oskar smiled at Phillip's transparent flattery. "I've had offers over the years. Mostly from businessmen who wanted to place it in a bank vault and let the violin sit there, un-played. They were only interested in letting the violin accrue in value."

"A caveat could be appended to the sale—a legal stipulation that qualifies the purchase."

Oskar slid the violin into the bag and carefully placed it in the case. He closed the lid and clicked shut the lock.

"I can take it to the auction house today," Phillip continued.

"Take it?" he replied. "I could never let this violin go."

The words made no sense. Had Oskar said *never*? thought Phillip. "You just mentioned that..."

"It's cold," Oskar said. "Throw a log on the fire."

Although Phillip estimated the room's temperature to be above seventy-five degrees, he acquiesced and slung a burl of oak on the fire. He rested a hand on the mantelpiece and watched the shower of sparks fly up. Soon he heard the reassuring pop and hiss of the dried sap meeting the flames. He turned to Oskar, who was fiddling with the lamp—flicking the switch on and off—and showed no interest in the fire or him. He thought of asking Oskar if he were all right or if he needed anything, even medication. That would be a bad idea, he knew. He left the room feeling more beguiled than before, and he looked for Anna in the hallway and the anteroom and then went up the stairs and called her name. He entered a high-ceilinged room with oak beams latticed in the corners and a glaze of white stucco on the walls. There was a single bed with a chintz duvet folded over to reveal pale lemon sheets, and a closet, the mirrored doors open, full of A-line dresses, frilly white blouses, and dark pantsuits. His interest was taken by a large bookshelf filled with records, and he flipped through the albums, seeing Oskar dolled up in black or spotlighted at the front of a seventy-piece orchestra. His hair was dark and thick and slicked straight back, and his face was serious as if he commanded the other musicians. When Phillip had finished with the records, he felt a great loss inside of him; a biting reminder that this was a life he could have led. He sat on the bed to rest for a moment and soon found himself smoothing down the duvet. There was a Haggadah on Anna's nightstand, he noticed, a deluxe Maxwell House edition printed on thick cardstock and enclosed within a blue cover. He flipped through the pages wondering how much of her Jewish past she embraced, if she thought about what her father had gone through in Czechoslovakia, and whether she was ever angry that he would not return to his homeland. Replacing the book, Phillip went to the window and saw Anna inspecting the stalks of a rosebush. She walked barefoot across the lawn to the thicket and leaned on one of the posts that marked the property boundary. She enjoyed the shade of a leafy hickory and the breeze that ran through her hair. When she turned, he jerked away from the window feeling guilty and went to his car.

* * *

Phillip pushed the MENU button on the remote and flipped through the channels, wasting time into the afternoon. He wanted to listen to music other than classical, to find a mess of contemporary cultural noise. Meaningless static. News about next year's millennium celebrations splashed across the screen. The program reported on what the future held for the country and how it would cope with a changing world. Soon he was sick of the talk of a new century, a new time—and he decided on an old-fashioned stroll, which, after, a three-block loop, returned him to the gift shop. The violin was gone. Phillip speculated it had been sold to a parent hopeful his child would turn out to be the next Mozart, even though it was the wrong instrument. The equating of classical music with the Austrian wunderkind had annoyed him for years and drew him to memories of his early career and Vanessa, whom he met at a college recital. In the campus chapel, she had approached him after his performance and told him how much she had enjoyed his delicate playing of Vivaldi's "Spring" concerto. They dated for eighteen months while he built his career: practicing for hours; attending rehearsals; performing at shows. Money was tight, yet he often thought of these moments as his happiest. Once they married, they lived off Buhrer Avenue in a Victorian house with a leaking asphalt roof. They rescued a patchy-haired Golden

48

Retriever from the pound and most mornings, before the city was awake, he would walk the dog to Tremont Park and let it run loose through the long grass. Vanessa would embrace Phillip when he returned, the leash wrapped tight around his wrist and the dog at his heel, and over breakfast they would plan, dream of their future together. How the years had slipped away, he was not quite sure. Vanessa still worked in medical billing, he knew, but at a new company in Columbus and she was now a regional manager. Even after their marriage ended they would talk every month or so, run through old times and then wait for the inevitable shift to how their lives were diverging. In their last telephone conversation she had asked why he was still alone, why he hadn't found anyone else. He had no answer for her and now as he drifted out of the gift shop, he recalled the kids in the neighborhood and his reputation as a loner.

He purchased a bottle of cheap Scotch at the corner liquor store and skulked back to the motel. Inside, his old suit hung off-kilter above the air-conditioning unit, the left shoulder erect from the wire hangar, while the right drooped and flapped in the frigid air. He questioned his impulse to have worn such a threadbare suit, and, annoyed at his self-pity, he ripped away the brown bag sheathing the bottle and twisted off the metal cap. Wistfully he sniffed the glass lip and gulped down two shots, enduring the burn in his throat and in the pit of his stomach. He was sick of his old suit, in the wallowing of his past, and he took it to the dumpster behind the motel. He tossed his jacket in first, then the pants. One leg hung out like a flattened dead eel. The idea came to him to light the pant cuff with his Zippo, and he watched the cotton smolder fiber by fiber into a glowing arc. He heard a shout from one of the motel rooms and in a panic he swatted at the small flame, feeling the crisp blistering of the charred cotton on his skin.

Later in the night a knock came on the door, and he opened it, slightly groggy and half-expecting to find the police. Anna was standing underneath the bright glare of the security light, which threw her face into sharp relief. She was wearing a hound's-tooth skirt cropped below the knee and a blouse with a shallow V that hid her cleavage.

"May I come in?" she said.

"Yes, if you'd like."

"I'm glad I caught you."

49

He offered her the room's sole chair and he went to his nightstand and quarter-filled two Styrofoam cups with Scotch.

"Thank you," she said, taking one cup.

"It's nothing special." He rubbed the red welt on the side of his hand and then feeling self-conscious sunk his hand into his pocket.

"I'm sure it's fine." Anna examined the exposed back panel of the painting above the bed. "Why is that picture turned around?"

"Bad art," he said, detecting the wisp of a smile on Anna's face. But then she closed her eyes, as if to purge his last words. When she reopened them, she dug out a tissue from her pocketbook. Her eyes were wet.

"I'm sorry about my father," she said, weighing the tissue in her hand. "The truth is we need to sell the violin to pay for his medical costs."

"My family went through something similar. They were tough times. If I can be of any help..."

"I don't need you to get mixed up personally with this. I just need a lump sum. The sooner, the better."

"I see," said Phillip.

Anna folded the tissue into a small square and tucked it under her cup. She touched her earlobe, massaging the gold stud between her thumb and forefinger. "This is an ugly room."

Phillip grinned. "It matches the painting."

"Will you come back?" she asked.

"I understand your situation, but I have business in Chicago."

"That's to be expected," she said, returning the cup.

"I can recommend someone."

"That would be helpful," she said, an air of regret coloring her words.

As Anna stood, Phillip smelled the jasmine soap on her skin and the sandalwood perfume on her nape. He missed the small touches that women enacted, the unconscious effort they went to. Anna's reluctance to accept his help beyond his middleman role frustrated him. Perhaps, he reasoned, he needed to approach the situation in a different way. "Do you want to go somewhere?" he asked. "Get a proper drink."

Her eyes looked directly into his and a shy smile curved her lips.

While they walked to a local bar, Anna worried aloud about her house—how she spent half the day cleaning it and dealing with the bills.

Her tone was matter-of-fact, the details just details, but now unloaded on a new audience. He listened respectfully, glad she trusted him enough to tell him her problems. At the end of Main Street, Phillip jerked his head toward the Landmark, a refurbished turn-of-the-century inn with lead glass windows and dull mahogany furniture. He ordered two Tom Collinses, and they sat at a booth overlooking the span of downtown stores.

"It's been a long time since I've been to a bar," Anna said, stirring her drink with a plastic mixing straw. The strong light revealed faint traces of acne scars on her cheeks and how she had tried to hide the marks with a fine, powdery foundation.

"Your father must keep you busy."

She picked up her glass, studied the tiny chip in its brim, and replaced it on the coaster. "I've been organizing his papers, trying to collect a record of his past."

"That's important," he said, sipping his drink. It was weak, and he wondered if the bartender had used rail gin.

"For him, that's true. I've wrestled with his past so long that I'm sick of it. My whole life has been about my father. I'm sorry. I shouldn't have said that."

"I'm not the judging sort."

"Truth be told, I should have left years ago. Even before his sickness, things weren't all right. He still treated me poorly—kept me on a tight leash. Of course, I've thought about leaving before. But it's too late now, and I don't want to worry him. He's given me so much, especially after Mother died. We traveled half the world together, and I have so many fond memories. Barcelona. Osaka. Milan." Anna smiled, almost apologetically, and then shook her head as if to dislodge her outward display of emotion. "Sometimes he mistakes me for Karolina. She's the lucky one. She lives in Texas and has a family of her own."

"Which part of Texas?"

Anna appeared not to acknowledge his question and her gaze focused on something out of the window. In front of the theater two young boys were slinging a baseball to one another. A woman of no more than thirty was studying the renovation schedule until she noticed the velocity of the ball, and she hustled the children away from the glass doors.

51

"The town looks different from here," she said, after a short while.

"It's no Chicago," he said, watching the boys obediently follow their mother.

Anna refocused on Phillip. "Do you like it there?"

"It's better than where I used to live. But big cities are big cities and I've lived in them all my life. They're what I know."

"I hope you stop by tomorrow."

"I can't promise anything."

Anna gazed down into the well of her drink. "I should go."

They strolled to the motel in silence. Anna went to her car and unlocked the driver's-side door. He stood there, hands behind his back. His head was buzzing from the alcohol. She came to him, kissed him on the cheek, her hands on his chest. He couldn't think of anything to say, and she got into her car and sped out of the parking lot. That night he slept in snatches. In his waking moments, he questioned whether Anna was attracted to him. Why had she kissed him? Was she thinking now about that moment too? If she had cared, he surmised, she would have said so. Or he would have. He tried to remember the first time Vanessa had been affectionate, when he was nineteen and had never been on a date. There was a movie theater and black coffee at a diner, and they had kissed in the gritted light of a train car and made love in the tiny apartment he rented on campus. Nothing else came to him, not what they had talked about underneath his sheets or how she had left his place and walked all morning. His memories were fading, like the wiped silver on a collection of antique Daguerreotypes, and he knew as he passed out that his life had fallen short.

* * *

A bank of thin cloud flattened the sky and left a gray light upon Phillip's view of the motel. He started his car, reversed out of the parking lot, and thought about his long drive to Chicago. He took a road that ran parallel to the river and saw the previous day's rain had formed a new stream. The swollen water rushed through the mud, turning rocks over, and carried away years of sedimented waste. If he ventured to Oskar's, he was unconvinced he would get the violin or even be recognized by Oskar.

He discerned, though, it was worth the effort to handle the Baron Knoop, and to talk again with Anna and to apologize for not having said anything.

Parking in the gravel drive, he saw Anna pruning a rosebush at the side of the house. She wore oversized khaki pants and a lime green sweater, her hands coddled in thick gardening gloves. She cut a half-dozen stems and snipped off the prickles. Her posture was stooped and, as she stood up straight, she held the small of her back and her face twisted into an ugly wince. Phillip stepped out of his car and waved. Anna bundled the flowers, along with the gloves, into a string bag and tossed the shears into a patch of dirt. She gestured to the porch, and he went over to meet her. At the doorway, she held the bag in front of her like a shield. She opened the door, allowing him to enter first, and then stamped her boots to rid them of the clogged earth.

Phillip was unsure what to say. As Anna came in, he stood still in an attempt to stall, to discover what was going on between them.

"The roses are late for the season," he said.

"We had an Indian summer."

"I have something for you," said Phillip, remembering.

"Oh?"

"To sign," he said, pulling out an envelope. "It's an insurance document for transporting the violin."

Anna opened the envelope and removed the letter. She scanned the words. Then she leaned the sheet of paper on the telephone stand and dashed off her signature.

"About yesterday," he said, folding the piece of paper and putting it inside his jacket pocket. "I'm not sure what I said..."

"Things, for me, are difficult."

"I understand."

She began to walk down the hallway. "We can talk about this later," she said.

Phillip followed her. "All right, but—"

Anna halted as though something had frightened her. Phillip was about to ask what was wrong, but he now realized she had heard the violin. The faint music was quiet and slow as if Oskar were building to something great, something transcendent. Phillip opened the French doors and looked in. Oskar was standing, his feet together and back straight, his eyes closed. He drew the bow slowly over the strings, caressing, almost languishing, in the beauty of the instrument. There was a slight shakiness to some of his bowing, tremors of doubt and fatigue vibrating through the air. Most of the notes were crisp and formed in Phillip's mind, drawing a sore lump in his throat, and for a few heartfelt seconds he tried to work out which piece Oskar was playing. His thoughts went to a libretto by a fellow Czech, Pavel Haas, and, as he tried to recall the name, Anna stood beside him—her breath on his neck. She linked fingers with his, and he felt she had roused from a deep slumber and made a choice. He tried to listen to the music, to confirm that his intuition was right, but he could only hear what Anna was saying, and he found himself repeating her words that this was a new beginning.

A Sky Green and Fields Blue

At the doorway to the barracks, Shoshana saw snow fall into the darkness. Now and then the searchlights scanning the camp illuminated the flurry of white, reminding her of the soap flakes her mother used to wash her clothes. She lifted the gauze from her wrist and picked at the scabby flesh that had grown over the blue numbers. She was tired of the factory, of the endless repetition, of the soreness and the bruises, the grease under her fingernails, the bread and lard rations that made her vomit, and the latrines smeared with dark liquid shit. Dafna, a Czech woman from Karlsbad, called her away from the door. Shoshana did not want to hear her words. She was tired of listening to the older women.

Two soldiers approached the barracks and entered through the rear door. She estimated one of the men was a clear six inches taller than the other, his posture ramrod-straight. He gripped the barrel and stock of his rifle as if ready to fight his way through the room and strode through the group of women sewing dresses, ignoring the cries of the sick, who held each other in their beds, trying to keep warm. The shorter soldier spoke to a dark Polish girl, who sat cross-legged on the floor, writing a letter. He said Shoshana's name, and the girl pointed her out.

Shoshana thought of running, but her legs deadened beneath her cotton-rag dress and she grasped at her gray bonnet, which hid the shame of her hair. The soldiers marched past the long row of double-tiered bunks, their jackboots thudding on the concrete. The first soldier ordered her to follow him, and she crouched down, petrified of what he wanted. She whispered, No...no, trying to find something to hold on to. He lifted her up by her spindly arms, and the shorter man barked *Jüdin* and pushed her through the door. Out in the night air she heard Dafna's broken German, her shouting at the soldiers to explain what was happening. The men did not reply and crossed the paved courtyard to a redbrick building,

55

Shoshana stumbling behind them. Her feet were cold in the snow, and she looked at the bloated gray clouds that threatened to bring in a winter storm. She was thankful the wind numbed her body, that she would not feel what was about to come.

The building was situated past a dozen other barracks and a guarded warehouse, which contained, she had been told, food and medicine. Unlike the barracks, the officers' quarters were warm and no draught circled through the paneled corridors. She was led into an office lit by the yellow flames of kerosene lamps. She had always disliked the burnt oil smell they produced and the difficulty of removing the liquid from clothes and bed linen. The soldiers left, allowing her a view of the dying embers glowing an unearthly red in the fireplace and a bookcase filled with dozens of large and important volumes, which were different to the paperbacks her family owned. Behind a large writing desk was a man she recognized as the Commandant. His shellacked salt-and-pepper hair was neatly parted on the right side and mirrored the rigid starch in his gray uniform. He was studying a series of documents fanned out on his desk and smoking a black-colored cigarette. After he signed the sheets and stacked them with care, he put the papers in the desk drawer and coughed into his fist. He stared at her until she blushed.

—Shoshana Meerapfel.

—Yes.

—You are from Berlin, correct? His voice was low-pitched, controlled. He held up an index card with four typed sentences on the front.

She opened her eyes further, trying to reason why her name was on the card. She nodded gingerly.

—Good. That explains certain qualities.

Shoshana was confused. She searched his face for clues, tracing the fine lines of his neatly trimmed beard, and settled on his clear blue eyes, which resembled a young boy's. His lips curled as he exhaled a long puff of gray smoke.

—I've been searching for girls like you, he said.

—For me?

—Let me see your hair.

Shoshana hesitated, and the Commandant grinned. He put down the index card and leaned back, his hands coming together on his chest.

—Before the war started, he said, I trained as an artist. Four years at the Karlsruhe Academy. I even exhibited at *Alte Staatsgallerie* and the *Kupferstichkabinett*. Several newspapers praised my paintings. I remember they said the girls were stripped of any modernist degeneration.

She did not know the meaning of his words, but she reasoned they described things cold and dark. He pointed to the oil paintings on the far wall, and she craned her neck to the four life-size portraits depicting girls around the same age as her. She guessed they were his daughters; the girls were thin and dressed in light blue frocks and had coifed blond hair cascading down their shoulders. A streak of jealousy ran through her, almost anger, and she imagined herself as one of the girls. She wanted their creamy skin and the deep rouge on their cheeks. She unknotted the straps of her bonnet, squashed the circle of soft cloth between her legs, and unclipped the brass pins that fastened her flaxen hair.

—*Danke*. You remind me of a girl I once knew in Linz, he said. She was very special.

—What was her name?

—Ida.

She smiled at the prettiness of the name.

—Do you like your hair? he asked.

—I don't understand.

—It is a simple question.

She thought her hair felt matted and smelled of the factory. She did not like the cheap fatty soap she had been given by Dafna. She knew the women in the barracks were curious as to why she was allowed to keep her hair. Some said she was too young for the barber. Others countered that assertion by noting her work in the factory. A few pestered her to explain why she had not been sent away with the other young girls.

—They make me wear a hat, she said. She held up the gray bonnet that she had tried to bury in her lap.

—They want to take your hair, shave it off, he said. He watched for her reaction, and when her eyes reddened, he continued: I want you to keep it. I want you to be like them. He gestured to the pictures.

Taking a second look, she noticed the girls had porcelain skin and bright eyes that contrasted with the dark forest in the background. Each painting was enclosed within a gilt frame, like the photograph her mother kept of her grandparents. The girl in the last picture entranced her. Her ringlets appeared spun from gold; her dress blue like summer sky. She pointed at the girl and said: My mother dresses me like that.

—That is Ida, he said, nodding. He appeared as though he were on the verge of saying something else, but then changed his mind.

—I used to have many dresses, she said.

—You will again.

—I would like that.

—Are you ready to be like Ida?

—I do not know.

—Do not be afraid, he said warmly.

He rose from his chair and closed the door to his office. From the corner of the room he dragged an armchair to where she was standing. The dark green upholstery appeared expensive, and she was scared the black lines of machine grease on her hands would stain the linen.

—Please, sit down, he said.

She perched on the edge of the seat cushion and leaned forward so she would touch very little of the green fabric. He stooped down; his face close to hers. She could smell heavy smoke on his breath and the faint trace of bergamot cologne. He snatched at her arm, but she pulled it to her chest, unwilling to be touched.

—Do not worry, he said. I will not hurt you.

She held out her arm, and the Commandant instructed her to sit properly in the chair. He posed her forearms on the smooth oak rests and studied the bandage that hid her infected tattoo. She thought there was discomfort in his face as he adjusted her sleeves to reach the top of her wrists. He reminded her of one of her uncles, the way he reluctantly washed her the day after Yom Kippur with a coarse rag. She felt distant from him now, more attuned to the warmth of the Commandant's fingers and his clean nails trimmed into smooth curves. Nervous, as he pushed her legs tightly together, she watched as he removed her brown leather shoes and put them by the door. The lice buried in the dirt between her toes embarrassed her, and she did not want him to see her this way; she wanted to be pure like her dress had once been.

—Look at me, he said; his voice direct and steady.

She lifted her eyes. His beard and moustache contained flecks of gray.

—Remove your star.

She tugged twice at the patch of yellow cloth, tearing the lapel of her dress to finally remove the star.

He reposed her arms and then sat behind his desk and sketched her for an hour. He said nothing the entire time, pausing only to drink coffee and to light another cigarette. He worked with a strange intensity, an acute gaze, which to Shoshana went beyond her cotton dress. It gave her an odd sense, one difficult to put into words. The Commandant reminded her of an older boy on the train to the camp who stared at her and continued to in Munich when the car filled with a dozen more Jewish families and he was squeezed against the planked side, boring his blunt eyes into her body. She remembered feeling sad, that he had wanted something from her, a part of her that she was willing to give. She searched for him after they were unloaded at the station. Men and women were divided into two separate groups. The women had gold jewelry taken and their shawl-bundles unraveled, the contents thrown into burlap sacks. At the same time, the men were kicked and spat on and herded into lines. Stripped of their wristwatches and Torahs, they were driven away in open-backed trucks. She had not seen the boy in the lineup and she wondered if he had been left behind in the cattle car.

The Commandant paused to examine his sketch. He drew his thumb across the paper and rubbed a section of the drawing. She tried to see what he had drawn, but he placed the sketchpad face down on the desk. He rested his elbows on the thick cardboard back and brought his hands to his forehead, stroking his temples in small circles. She blamed herself for not being pretty enough. He will like me better in a blue cotton dress, she thought, trimmed with white lace. She leaned forward to say those words, but he stood and stepped over to the fireplace.

—Is it cold in here? he asked, lowering his hands to the ashes.

—No.

He opened a circular tin on the mantel and took out a large brown segment, which she was pleased to see was chocolate. He broke the slab in two and put one half in her hand and returned the rest to the tin. She clasped the chocolate tightly and felt the smudge of warmth.

—Tomorrow, he said. You will come back tomorrow.

* * *

Lying in bed, Shoshana played with the pleats of her dress. It was colored dun-brown, but she could tell it had once been bright white. She recalled the odor of bleach when she helped her mother with the laundry, adding starch to the water, running clothes through the mangle, and folding each blouse and dress into a pristine square. She could not re-collect how long ago that was, only that her mother sent her to live with relatives in the country, a house later raided by men in heavy, gray uniforms. Perhaps she had been in the camp less than a month. Time was hazy. Yet she knew she had turned twelve a few days before and was younger than the other girls. Her breasts were still thin and small, and one girl teased her because she still had not bled.

Sometimes she thought she could see the faint outline of flowers in her dress, curved lines that Dafna pointed out were just dirt rings. Dafna had a shaven head covered with a Tichel, like the other married women. She also had a toothless mouth that had been fitted with gold fillings. She told Shoshana the day she arrived at the camp, soldiers pulled out her teeth with an iron wrench. When Shoshana was assigned to her barracks and to her bunk, a plank shelf topped with a rag blanket, Dafna said she was the mother to anyone who had lost hers. Shoshana was not sure what Dafna meant by that. She knew her own mother would be arriving on next week's train.

Dafna marched to the bunks at the far end of the room. A gong was rung. Shoshana remained still, not wanting to rise. The women next to her went to the latrines or boiled water for tea. She did not want to get up and go out into the frozen dark of the morning. She remembered the warmth of the Commandant's office, as if the heat from the embers had washed over her. She eyed the women milling around the iron stove, gulping down the clear liquid and wiping their thin lips with a shared rag. She covered her face with her hands, unable to watch them anymore. Then she felt a cutting pressure on her wrist.

—Get up, said Dafna. Her eyes were tar black.

—Yes, replied Shoshana.

From outside a shrill guard whistle sounded and the barks of Alsatians rumbled through the barrack's walls. She slipped down from her bunk, shivering in the chill air. Avoiding Dafna's gaze, she put on her shoes and went to the doorway. She braced herself for the snow, folded her arms over her chest, and followed the women to a gravel road and onward to the waiting trucks. Two soldiers flanked the women: the men trod in step, automatic rifles slung over their shoulders. A dour-faced officer, shivering in the cold, marked the women in his black leather notebook and read off the assigned vehicles. Shoshana counted thirty women in her truck. Some talked Yiddish, others German, and a group at the end she guessed were speaking in Polish. She squeezed in next to Dafna, who spoke to the three Czech girls in front of her.

—Today, we must work hard, said Dafna.

The truck sped down the road and stopped at the steel gates, where a solider briefly inspected the women and then waved them on. The land outside the camp flattened into a sea of snow, and Shoshana imagined the waves of white crashing onto the forest shore. The watchtowers, and the machine guns sighted on the women, drifted away into a series of far-off islands. Her eyes closed as she tried to ignore Dafna's observations about the approaching brick buildings and the three tall chimneys. She had seen the structures numerous times before and she was tired of the same talk. When she did look out, she saw a group of laborers carrying tools into the entrance of the largest building. Dafna spat onto the truck bed and inched forward to spy on the men, trying to determine what they were doing. We *must* work hard, she repeated. We *must* endure. She lowered her head and carried on talking about her family and her hope they had survived the raids of the S.S.

It was less than a kilometer to the factory, and Shoshana heard the thrum of the machines inside: a loud pulsing sound interspersed with metallic crashes, as though a large hammer were constantly being raised and smashed down onto an anvil. She could not imagine how she heard the other women's voices each day and she feared she might go deaf. The truck braked hard outside of the factory. Each of them read the metalwork sign: ARBEIT MACHT FREI. Shoshana wanted to believe in the idea of work setting you free. She had labored for her mother as long as she could remember, helping with the sewing business run from their home. Several times a day women stopped by with suits in need of repair and instructions for fashioning wedding dresses and winter drapes from bolts of cloth and silk. But that routine seemed so far in the past now and her thoughts switched to the Commandant and the chocolate he had given her. She was ravenous for more; she dreamed she would not have to go to the factory each morning, but visit his office and sit in the chair to be drawn.

Fluorescent lights hung from skeletal steel beams and cast a murky glow across the assembly lines. Two long lines of women flanked the wrought iron machines, which Dafna once told Shoshana existed to produce aircraft parts for the bombers. The conveyer belt hummed as it cranked giant shards of metal along, and Shoshana disliked the women's slack skin and hollow cheeks, and their bulging eyes focused on assembling the pieces. Her job was to fetch tools for the women or to pick up lost bolts. As she worked, she saw men from the other half of the camp at the next line. One man with a balding pate and arms raw with scabies collapsed to the ground. A soldier shouted at him to rise. When the man grasped at the soldier's boots, the soldier struck him with the butt of his rifle. Through the day women were taken away and would return with bloodied faces and large tears in their dresses. She feared the same would happen to her. So when the guards passed, she made sure she was carrying a wrench set or sweeping the factory floor.

* * *

In the afternoon, Dafna tugged Shoshana's sleeve and gestured to the Commandant entering their section of the factory. Shoshana admired his slim build and the polished silver buttons on his gray tunic. A rumor spread that he was inspecting the factory to make sure the production targets were on schedule. With the head of the work detail and the female attendant, he toured the assembly line and asked questions and pointed at the machines and the workers. She watched him listen intently to each of his staff, making notes in a leather-bound notebook, his pencil scratching at the paper as though he were still sketching her.

After evening roll-call, the women trudged to the factory's makeshift canteen. Shoshana guessed it had existed once as a storage facility. There were rows of tables, and wooden barrels that held aluminum bowls and cups. The women picked up their bowls and cups and took them to the food station where haggard women with rawboned arms dished out stale bread, alongside greasy slivers of rancid lard, and ladles of watery meat stew. She sat at the table with Dafna and the other Czech girls. Their hands were raw and nicked with cuts and scrapes. She did not feel hungry; she felt numbed by the hard labor.

—You must eat, said Dafna.

Shoshana's head dropped and she began to cry. I want my mother, she said.

Dafna settled her arm on Shoshana's back and rubbed the soft skin between her shoulder blades. Dafna told her of family dinners, how she sat with her two daughters and ate *česneková polévka*, a rich, garlic soup and a course of *houskové knedlíky*, which she explained were potato flour dumplings.

—It is good to eat, she said.

Shoshana picked the black mold from her bread, thinking of past meals she shared with her mother and then of reasons why the Commandant had not spoken to her. She considered he had been preoccupied with the production targets or that he had found another girl from one of the neighboring barracks. She glanced at Dafna slurping the stew from her spoon. She wanted to tell her about the Commandant's work, his life as an artist and his painting of Ida, but she could see in Dafna's eyes that she would not understand.

* * *

Over the next few days, a winter storm submerged the camp in a thick blanket of snow. Shoshana studied the pine forest that covered the hills in the distance. The jagged points zigzagged across the sky, as if hiding a secret. She had heard of a path, a route out of the area. A handful of Jews, she had been told, had escaped. Found a way home. She liked that the trees were similar to the ones surrounding her relatives' country house. She recalled climbing a mature alder with two of her cousins and ~asping at the sloping, leafy branches, which separated the tree from the ~unding pine. Now, as she realized the similarity between the forest

63

and the backdrop of the Commandant's paintings, she placed herself inside one of his landscapes, lovingly foregrounded in a lavish silk dress, and the Commandant painting her.

The light steadily diffused behind thickening clouds and the land darkened. Guards marched into the courtyard with a group of prisoners and ordered them to clear a series of paths between the buildings. Uninterested in the men, she focused on the smokestacks. Strange patterns emerged in the snow stuck to the sides of the chimneys. Whorls of a great fingerprint transformed into the outline of her mother's face: her sharp eyes and her narrow, birdlike nose. She wondered where her mother was and what she was doing. Dafna had said her mother had not been on the last train.

In bed that night, the women who flanked her could not sleep because of hunger pains. They huddled together in a ball of ragged cotton and naked flesh. She drank their breaths and deep moans, reliving how the Commandant locked his eyes on her. Yet she did not understand why his presence drew an uneasy feeling, why her stomach hurt for him. To her relief, after the blizzard had settled in the morning, the Commandant sent his men to escort her to his office. She was glad to go back and rest in a place of warmth. The chair was in the middle of the room, but she dared not sit. She waited for his instructions. As he retrieved his sketchpad from his desk, he told her of his life before the war. He recounted stories of the women he had known and the daughters he had immortalized.

—I captured Ida at her pinnacle, he said. That summer in Linz, I could have painted her every day.

She detected an ache of sadness in his voice. I miss my mother, she said.

—Not your father?

—I do not remember him. He died when I was very young. She glanced at the paintings and lowered her eyes, afraid to meet his gaze. Where is Ida?

—She died of tuberculosis, he said, resting the sketchpad on his legs. But I refuse to think of such things. He stood and went to his bookshelf. His forefinger traced across the spines until he picked out an exhibition catalogue. He crouched down next to Shoshana so they were of equal height. She read the title, *Entartete Kunst*. The cover bore a picture of a sculpted African face with a flat, wide nose and thickly curved lips. The distorted features were strange and new to her, and she wanted to see more. She turned the pages and let her fingers hover over the black-and-white images, as if she could absorb the works of art.

—The imagination is abhorrent, he said, pointing to a painting of crippled German soldiers. She had never seen a picture like this before, the crude lines of color and the angular bodies. The men looked cartoonish and weak as they paraded through a city street. Yet she did not understand his words, the reasons why he hated these images.

—Why?

His face reddened, and he ran his hand through his short, gelled hair. He answered: It leads to a perversion of the real. As the Führer wrote, you cannot have an artist who paints a sky green and fields blue.

She giggled at the idea of the reversed colors until she noticed the anger in his gaze, and she became terrified that she had done something wrong.

—It is degenerate art. The artist of such things ought to be sterilized and his work destroyed. He closed the catalogue and stormed over to the paintings on the wall. This is beauty, he said.

Shoshana was confused by his ire and his words. Her eyes welled up.

—Tears will not help you, he said, or your people. He continued to stare at the painting of Ida and in a calm voice said, Please sit.

She settled on the chair and removed her shoes, ready to be drawn.

Over the next few hours, he positioned her in different poses. He stood her up with her arms loose by her side and then he got her to kneel with her hands clasped in prayer. None of his drawings satisfied him, and she wondered why he wanted her in his pictures. She was grateful, though. After he drew her, he gave her a bowl of hot vegetable broth and a cup of chicory coffee splashed with cognac.

* * *

That night, in the barracks, Shoshana lay on her hardwood bed replaying the taste of the food the Commandant had given her. Her tongue was burnt from the hot coffee, but she did not mind. She wanted more of the rich, woody flavor.

65

Dafna walked past her bunk and said Shoshana was becoming fat, that she had a glow of health not experienced by the other girls.

—What are they feeding you? she demanded. You should share any food you receive.

—Nothing. I do not receive anything.

—Your arms, legs, belly, are fat, she said. Dafna grabbed at Shoshana's dress and tried to lift it up.

—Stop, please, said Shoshana. She was scared of Dafna and scared of the Commandant. She felt though they shared something special and that he was different to other men: the soldiers, and her uncles, and the rabbis in her neighborhood. She edged herself to the far side of the bed, and wrapped her blanket around her shoulders. I will give you whatever I get, she screamed.

Dafna grabbed Shoshana's foot and pulled her off the mattress to the floor. Shoshana cried out and kicked Dafna's shins, leading Dafna to bat Shoshana's legs to the side and snatch her bonnet, holding it as if it were a prized jewel. She called to one of the Czech girls for a pair of scissors, and the girl retrieved them from a narrow gap between two bunks. Dafna dragged Shoshana to a chair and signaled the girl to hold Shoshana's arms. Shoshana struggled, but she had no strength in her body. The steel blades glided through her hair. Blond locks fell in clumps to the planked floor. She wept for her mother.

—She is not coming, said Dafna.

—She promised.

Dafna shook her head.

Shoshana surveyed the room to see if any of the other women would help her. But most were sleeping in the bunks, too tired to move.

—This is for your own good, explained Dafna. The women are envious.

—No! Shoshana screamed and twisted her neck, trying to avoid the slashing of her hair. She stopped when she saw Dafna had tears in her eyes and she let her head loll to the side, to let Dafna cut, to make her the same as the other women.

When Dafna finished, she passed the scissors to the Czech girl. Shoshana slouched forward into Dafna's arms, and Dafna cradled her and stroked her back. She sang a Czech nursery rhyme that Shoshana could not translate, whispering the chorus into her ear, telling her that her own mother used to sing it years before. When Dafna released her, she slunk to her bed and cried all night, not sleeping. Her hair had been reduced to tufts barely an inch long. She kept a handful of the locks under her thin pillow and ran her thumb over the greasy clumps, caressing the strands until dawn.

* * *

The following day Shoshana was not summoned to see the Commandant. Perhaps, she thought, he had caught the influenza that was spreading through the camp and had wanted time to recuperate. By the evening she was scared that he had found out about her hair. It was a blessing, she reasoned, when the soldiers came for her in the early morning. At first she struggled with them, in a show of pretense for the other women. When she saw Dafna was asleep, she relented and let them drag her outside.

The Commandant had brought a *méridienne* into his office. Taken from Paris, he boasted. He had arranged it against the wall with three silk pillows and a plain wool blanket. He instructed her to lie down. As she did so, he wiped the wet gloss from his forehead and picked up a leather-bound book from his chair. He flipped through the pages to show her a nineteenth-century painting titled, *"Dornröschen."* The girl in the picture was sleeping supine on a bed, and Shoshana was immediately enamored with the girl's beauty. Her delicate head rested on her fleshy forearm and a rouge-colored velvet blanket covered her pale body.

—Be like this, he said.

She lay down on the *méridienne* and arranged herself into the pose and drew the blanket over her chest.

—One day I will use oils, he said, to capture you.

She removed her bonnet and closed her eyes, curious as to the intensity of the moment. She lay down and crossed her arms, finding her own flesh to be the softest she had ever felt. Her fingertips danced over a dry patch of skin that she rubbed and rubbed. She glimpsed down to see what marred her wrist and she saw that the Commandant had not opened his sketchpad.

—What is this? he asked.

The revulsion in his face alarmed her. He went over and knelt at her side, pawing her bare scalp, and running his fingers over the soft bumps and shallow grazes.

—I saved you from the barber. Are you not thankful?

She clasped her hands to her cheeks and then drew her fingers together in front of her mouth. She wanted to speak, to explain to him what had happened, tell him that her hair would grow back and he could draw her again. But the words would not come.

The Commandant's head dropped and he went to the door. He turned and threw his sketchpad, and she, in return, raised her arms to protect her face. The sheaf of papers ricocheted off her wrists and the sheets scattered to the floor. She stared at the detailed pencil drawings of her face and body. The beauty he saw in her astonished her. Her cheeks were plump and her eyes were clear. But something about the sketches did not make sense.

—This is Ida, she said.

—*Geh weg*, he spat. His face reddened and he removed his peaked cap to wipe the sweat from his forehead. He replaced his cap and smoothed down the creases on his tunic. He opened the door to his office and called in the guards, ordering them to take her away. They grabbed her arms and hauled her out of the room. Her bare feet dragged on the floorboards in a last effort to stay. The taller guard pushed open the door and a blast of icy wind struck them.

—Wait, she said. Wait.

The guard balanced himself on the steps and shielded his eyes. He led Shoshana into the courtyard. Her thin wrist slipped from his grip and suddenly there was a short distance between them. The second guard sneered and kicked her in the stomach, and she crumpled into the ash-colored snow, holding her bruised abdomen. He ordered her to the barracks. As she stood, she saw across the courtyard the electrified fence at the camp's perimeter and the wooded hills beyond. She spun around, searching for a world beyond the Commandant's. She wanted to escape, to get away from the camp and the factory. She imagined the path in the forest and the dirt trail snaking back to her home and to her mother cleaning clothes in the laundry. Her mother rose from her stooped position and beckoned Shoshana to bring over the bleach. She could see her mother's face against the white sheets, smiling and then vanishing as a terrible burnt smell seeped from her body. At first Shoshana thought she smelled the kerosene from the Commandant's office. Then, as she staggered back to the barracks, she noticed the thick clouds overhanging the smokestacks and the sky changing to a blackened green.

Firelight

By August 1959, Father had worked for thirty-five years in the insurance business. He sold property and life policies to neighborhood families, to burly mechanics at the gasoline stations on the Lower East Side, and to stenographers down at the courthouse. Each premium earned him a bonus, which he saved for our new Cape house in Levittown. The place had recently been re-painted a pale green to keep it in line with the other houses in the neighborhood. The lawn, though, was overgrown, potted with Bermuda grass and molehills. The previous owners had split to Florida and left the realtor to take us around the property. Connected to the dull Formica kitchen was a pastel living room with a redbrick fireplace choked with soot. As Father and the realtor pored over the bathroom and the two small bedrooms, I stared at the Admiral TV inserted into the wall under the staircase. The gray screen was barely six inches across and coated in a fine dust. I fiddled with the knobs, attempting to turn it on.

"William, leave that alone," Father said, reentering the room. "That's expensive."

Though I was seventeen, Father treated me like a kid. He hadn't always, but since my mother died in a car accident he had distanced himself. Weeks before, after talking the situation through at the funeral with a cloistered group of relatives, he decided to relocate us to the suburbs in Long Island and sell insurance to the local housewives. "There's good money in it," he told me. We packed her clothes and shoes and her favorite lavender soaps and medicinal salves. He neatly labeled the large cardboard boxes, squaring off each edge, and drove us to a church in Weehawken. We stacked them one by one near the entrance. He tried to move quickly, but his Sears & Roebuck suit hampered his movement and revealed the girth of his body. I cried each time I put a box by the door and

71

saw the cross carved into the lintel. When we finished, he combed his short gray hair to the side and said we should leave.

During the first days in the new house he left early for work, surveying the neighborhood for potential leads. The move to Levittown meant I switched high schools and left my friends behind. They said they would keep in touch, but Father wouldn't install a telephone until Nixon won the election years later. I tried reasoning with him, but he insisted the peace and quiet would leave us with time to reflect. I spent my time next to the empty pool in the backyard, trying to survive the wilting heat. My legs hung over the curb and I wrote letters to my friends and a girl, Cindy, I had once taken on a date to see *Some Like It Hot*. After the movie we had shared a soda and French kissed until her curfew.

When school started I tried to forget it was my senior year. I didn't want to think about selling insurance with Father post-graduation. We had agreed, though, on the drive to Levittown that it was the best thing for me. As the moving van pulled up outside the new house, I already regretted my passive, "Sure, Dad."

Our relationship began to change when I discovered avant-garde and foreign literature in my English class. The teacher, who asked us to call him Peter, was straight out of a college somewhere in California. He wore a rumpled corduroy suit, and when he was sure the Principal had completed his rounds, he replaced his shoes with moccasins and wrenched off his navy blue necktie. Each day he read epic poems, like Homer's *The Iliad* or Ovid's *Metamorphoses*, and when he was spent, he asked us our opinions and our philosophies on life. Sometimes the class was shocked at the things we discussed, but no one ever complained. We all secretly looked forward to his sharp dissection of art and passionate speeches about books we had never taken note of in our previous classes.

* * *

One Friday afternoon, in the last class of the week, I sat at my desk sweating heavily. Warm air was coming through the window that faced a small grass field. Outside, a class of freshman was performing jumping jacks. Their teacher kept shouting, "Jump!" every time they paused. One girl was bent double as though she had a cramp, and behind her a stocky blond boy swatted at the black flies. In the classroom, the other students were fanning themselves with their notebooks and staring at the clock above the blackboard. We had been learning about Tolstoy and Chekhov, but none of us could connect to their world.

Peter circled the room, reading aloud from his anthology of Russian writers. He wore khaki pants without a belt, which meant he tugged them up after he finished each page. His hands and face were a tanned brown, a similar honey color as my mother's. I knew she grew up in Santa Rosa, and I wondered if he had ever visited the city. "Ignore them outside. Imagine the Russian winter," he said, returning to the lectern. He wrote Лёв Николáевич Толстóй on the blackboard and stared at his handiwork for a few seconds. "It's a hard language. Difficult to understand."

A girl near the front raised her hand. "What does that mean?"

Peter gave her a toothy smile. "That's Tolstoy's name in Russian." He removed a postcard from his anthology and held it up. On the front was a drawing of a young boy in a spaceship, circling the Earth. He wore an orange spacesuit and was waving to an unseen person. In the background were red and white stars and a smattering of Cyrillic letters that Peter translated as, "Happy New Year."

He gave the postcard to a boy to his left and asked him to pass it around the class. "Last summer," he continued, "I wrote to one of Tolstoy's distant cousins. I wanted to learn more about Tolstoy's last days. The cousin told me about an occasion his father had visited Tolstoy at Yasnaya Polyana, the family estate. It had been a long, cold winter and the snow had compacted into a thick ice sheet. In the study, he found Tolstoy burning a stack of unpublished stories to keep warm. He ran over to try and save them. However, Tolstoy waved the man off and said, 'God is in these pages, but I'm not worthy to see him.'"

When I got the postcard, I studied the strange writing for a long time. It was an unusual tale, and I wasn't sure what it meant or even if he had correctly translated the Russian. At home, I decided to grow my hair like Peter's and keep the top of my shirt unbuttoned. In my room, I read stories and poems he had recommended to me after class: Kerouac, Ginsberg, Ferlinghetti. The only thing Father read was the daily copy of the *Herald Tribune* he picked up from the diner on Hicksville Road. He kept the newspapers stacked on the kitchen table and then reread them every Sunday, as though he were reliving the entire week.

Father even worked on Saturdays, trying to convince our neighbors in the adjoining cul-de-sacs that life was unthinkable without fully comprehensive policies. He quoted the death rates of the middle classes and the prevalence of home accidents, and he handed out free pamphlets with titles such as *Protecting Your Family in the Nuclear Age* and *Quit Gambling, Start Insuring*. When he came home, I would hear him slump in his chair and watch game shows until he passed out. Often I found him asleep, his fat body in repose with his shirt open, his socks and shoes discarded, and his feet in a large bowl of ice.

One night Father woke me with his snoring, which I could hear was coming from the living room. I got up and slipped on my robe. His bowl of ice had melted and spilled onto the floor. He was sleeping in his chair, hands on the smooth armrests, and his head lolled back as if ready for an executioner. His red and sunburned face seemed angry, and I wondered what was taking place in his dreams.

"Dad," I said. He didn't stir. So I squeezed his shoulder. "Time for bed."

He grumbled something I couldn't quite hear. Then he said: "It's early."

"There's water on the floor."

He glanced at the dark stain on the carpet. "It will dry."

"Mom wouldn't let you lay here."

He leaned forward and rubbed his temples. "I suppose you're right," he said drowsily, and retired to his room.

* * *

Over the following weeks I spent more time in my room, hunched at my desk, reading books ordered through the mail. Between stories, I gazed at the backyard and the pool slowly filling with orange and brown leaves. Beyond the pool was a large grassy area, where children played Cowboys and Indians or built a fort out of pressed-metal lawn chairs and white linen sheets. One hot afternoon I joined them and we dug a shallow trench, pretending we were soldiers on Omaha Beach. A young boy said I was their general, and I led them across the grass to war. That evening

I read *On the Road* for the first time and imagined myself as Kerouac's Sal Paradise, leaving behind the places where he grew up. There was vitality in the prose, a dynamism that led me to read the book in one sitting. All night I reveled in the manic descriptions of bebop, the round-the-clock parties and wine-fueled philosophizing, and then I thought of the road to California, and how, and why, my mother ended up in New York.

After Kerouac, I bought more books and invested in a library membership, filling my room with anything that was set out-of-state. I copied out passages of Tolstoy's *The Death of Ivan Ilyich* and tried to understand why he destroyed his own work. Eventually I progressed to writing my own fiction, usually stories of suburban escape or heroic journeys to the West Coast. I showed them to Peter, and he smiled at the thick stack of paper. He asked if he could take them and see what I was writing about.

Almost a month later, as class ended, he called me over. He seemed tired. His eyes were glazed and underlined by purple crescents. He removed his jacket, and I saw sweat patches on the sides of his blue shirt.

"Your stories," he said, "there's passion in them."

"They're terrible. I never write what I want to say."

He looked me in the eye. "You've got talent." He brought out my stories from his brown leather satchel and read a few lines from one of them. He leaned back on his heels as he mouthed the words, his lips breathing new life into the characters. "This is great work," he said, showing me the page he was on. "You have many strong ideas in here, and I really like your descriptions of the landscape. This Eddie is quite a character."

"Thank you."

"Say, what are your plans after graduation?"

"A job," I said, still a little in shock that he liked my stories. "Dad can fix me up at Metropolitan. Selling insurance."

"How about college?"

"Too expensive for Dad. Besides, I'm not sure I'd fit in."

"You can get a scholarship," he said.

"I don't have the smarts."

"You're brighter than you think," he said. "I'll write you a letter of recommendation."

As the semester drew on, Peter sketched out a plan of action. I was to apply to an upstate liberal arts college. He told me I could major in English literature or something else, something I loved. He also knew a friend in the town that could get me a part-time job at an Italian restaurant, washing dishes and chopping vegetables. "It's settled," he said. I had a vague idea that I would travel to California before college began the next fall and visit the areas I had read about. I wanted to climb the Matterhorn Peak and squat in North Beach coffee houses, reading poetry until the sun set over the wharf.

* * *

In our old house, my mother and I used to sing Kitty Wells' "Lonely Side of Town" together. She had a much better voice and knew the lyrics of all her favorite songs. While she ironed Father's shirts, I completed my math homework. Since the move, I kept her collection of country records at the bottom of my closet—twenty-three LPs wrapped in a bed sheet. When I pulled them out, I liked to look at the pictures of women in cotton gowns on the covers and remember the ones she wore. On top of the records was my college acceptance letter. I hadn't told Father about my college plans and my desire to travel out West.

On the Thursday of Thanksgiving, I lay in bed most of the day and listened to some of her records. I had been feeling sad the entire morning, glaring at my reflection in the black vinyl discs, and even rereading some Kerouac had not helped. By the evening I felt lousy and didn't want to talk to anyone. As I dreaded, Father called me into the kitchen. On the table he had set dinner out. Sweating in a baking dish was a meatloaf end. In two sky blue bowls were mashed potato and green peas with sour cream.

"I'm not much of a cook," he said, fixing me a plate.

"It's O.K., Dad."

"Next year, things will be better." He pointed to a china teacup half-hidden behind his stack of newspapers. "Gravy, if you want it." He cut up his meatloaf and ate a greasy sliver. He chewed for a long time, as though the gristle were unwilling to leave his mouth. As he drove his fork into a second chunk of meatloaf, he noticed I was not touching my food.

"I got these potatoes from the yard," he said. "This whole town used to be potato fields."

"I'm not hungry."

He put down his knife and fork. "In that case, listen. I've set up an interview with Metropolitan," he said, waiting for a response. When none materialized, he continued: "Just wear your suit, answer their questions the best you can, and the job's yours."

"I don't graduate for months."

"You need to prepare for your future."

"I'm not sure I want to—"

"William, it's good money."

"You don't understand."

"I understand plenty."

"You've never asked me what I want." His face curled as I poured gravy on my meatloaf. I couldn't tell if he was angry or surprised, but I knew I had the advantage. "There are things out there that I want to see."

He scrutinized me for a few seconds and then shook his head. He wiped his lips with his napkin, tossed it onto his plate, and drew back from the table. He went to his bedroom and returned with a cream-colored sports jacket that I had not seen before. As he put it on, he said, "Nothing out there you don't have already." He brushed past me and out of the door.

* * *

For a couple of days, Father barely spoke. When he was home, he barreled through the house fixing leaking faucets and removing soot from the fireplace. By the backdoor he found an ant's nest and doused it with boiling water. To escape his moods, I took strolls in the neighborhood. I threaded through the long, curving streets that looped at the ends. The houses on either side were not as identical as I had first thought. Some had their carports converted into a study or a nursery, others simply a garage. Several houses had large additions to the side or rear, sunrooms for the husbands to read the newspaper or for the wives to knit woolen scarves and hats for the upcoming winter.

I kept my walks to the patchwork of communal backyards, dotted with mud piles and lost toy guns and Indian headdresses. At the rear of each house were concrete patios and flowerbeds that gradually faded into the grass. If I kept to the blurry edges of the backyards, I could see clearly into the neighbors' houses. At least half were empty, but several had children at the window. A few stuck their tongues out; some waved, some barely noticed me. At the end of the cul-de-sac was the grandest building on the street. It was a new ranch house with a split roof and a double-size carport. The living room had a large picture window and powder blue drapes. Through the small gap, I glimpsed Father talking to a woman in a teal dress. Her bust was clearly visible, outlined against the shear of the cotton, and, aside from my tumescent swelling, I wasn't sure I should keep staring. They both were sitting on a sectional couch. She vaguely resembled my mother. Her curled hair was short in the front and long in the back, and my initial attraction dissipated. My father pointed to the pamphlet she held in her hand. She seemed nervous and kept pushing an imaginary lock from the side of her face. They talked for a few minutes and finally they both stood. As he left the room, he kissed her on the cheek.

When he came home that night, I threw down my book and went to the living room. Father had fixed himself a tall glass of whiskey packed with ice. His new sports jacket hung on the coat rack by the door, and his briefcase was open on the coffee table. He took out his pamphlets, arranged them into discrete piles, and scrawled a note in his ledger.

I sat on the couch and leafed through an old copy of *Life Magazine*. I read a photo essay entitled, "How the West was Won" and marveled at the pictures of pine forests and grassy plains. I wanted to ask him about the woman, but wasn't sure how to broach the subject.

"Have you read this article?" I said, brandishing the magazine.

Without looking he answered, "No."

"How was work today?"

"A lot of walking, a few sales." He counted the pamphlets one more time and then replaced them in his briefcase. He finished his whiskey, switched on the TV, and settled back in his chair. The slow burn of static emerged on the screen and developed into a fuzzy picture of a man. He wore black-rimmed glasses that emphasized his large forehead and the remains of his dark hair, which was slicked to the right. In the background were household items—fridge, stove, dining set—with signs printed with cash values.

"No sound again." He sighed. "I like this show."

"Did Mom ever go back and visit California?"

He rose from his chair and fiddled with the dial. "Have you touched the TV?"

"Dad."

"What?"

"I saw you talking to someone. A woman."

"Oh," he said.

"Are you dating her?"

He turned around. "I love your mom."

"You never talk about her."

"I don't have time. I work."

"Who is she?"

"Who's who?"

"The woman in the teal dress."

"A client."

On my daily walks I never saw him at the house again, though I did see the woman once more. She was sitting alone on the couch and wearing a black gabardine dress. She read a slick magazine and then painted her nails blush-red. I sat down in the long grass and watched her bake brownies in the kitchen. She reminded me of my mother and the time we had spent frosting a birthday cake for Father.

* * *

Over the Christmas break, an aunt and uncle—I recognized them from the funeral—drove in from Wisconsin. They were the last relatives alive on Father's side. For ten days we listened to their anecdotes about our family and their complaints about the lack of plush carpeting and hot water in the house. In the evenings, we played backgammon and Parcheesi and ate small bowls of my aunt's Jell-O salad. My uncle moaned about his wretched kidneys and his job with the railroad. I had nothing to add. Seeing their faces brought back the emotions of the funeral. Father appeared restless, as though he yearned to head out with his briefcase full of policies. Nothing was said about my mother, although I overheard them mention my name multiple times. Usually they presumed I was out of earshot or not listening to their conversation. One evening, while they drank sherry and took down the last of the Christmas decorations, my uncle cornered Father in the living room.

"What about the boy?" he said.

"He doesn't need to know the details."

"It was a sorry business."

Father looked to the fireplace and drained the last of his sherry.

"And the job?" my uncle pressed.

"He'll do fine. It's good work. It will make a man of him."

They became quiet when I entered from the kitchen. I nodded respectfully and picked up a cardboard box filled with paper snowflakes.

"What are the details?" I asked.

My aunt, who sat knitting, glowered at me and then at Father.

"Tell him," my uncle said.

Father led me into the backyard. The ground was covered with a hard frost that made a crunching sound as we walked toward the pool. I wasn't sure what he was going to tell me, though I knew it would involve my mother. He didn't look my way until we reached the curb and then he gave me a pained smile. We stood there for a long time not saying anything. We could hear the distant cries of children playing and then high-pitched voices calling them in for dinner.

"Son, I've kept something from you," he said at last. "When she died she was leaving the city, moving back to Santa Rosa."

"Why?"

"Things weren't working out."

I shivered and crossed my arms to keep warm. "It's cold out here."

He hooked his arm around me, and we trudged back into the house. Inside, my uncle was shoveling coal onto the fire and my aunt was steeping hot tea in the kitchen. I said I was tired and went to my room. Really, I was sad. If what Father said was true, I wanted to know why my mother hadn't told me and why she hadn't made plans for me to relocate to Santa Rosa. I tried to read, to take my mind off the subject. I just stared at the pages. In the night I heard raised voices. My aunt asked to see the family Bible and Father said it had been lost in the move. "You're trying to forget us," she screamed. The reply from Father was muffled as he, or my uncle, switched on the TV. The next day, when my aunt and uncle left for Wisconsin, they said they would write to me, but no letter ever arrived.

* * *

A Nor'easter billowed two feet of snow on Levittown soon after, swamping the roads and preventing Father from going to work. He took to drinking in the morning. I could smell whiskey in every room. When he went to the backyard to smoke, I found used glasses, not even rinsed, on the sideboard and on the coffee table. One morning I followed a trail of melted snow to the kitchen. Through the window I saw him next to the pool, using it as an ashtray. He was facing the house of the woman who wore the teal dress. He stood there and finished the whole pack and then came back inside and told me it was bedtime.

When the snowplows bulldozed through our neighborhood, Father eyed them from the doorway—his briefcase in hand. He trailed one of the trucks up the street, pacing hard behind it. I was glad that school had started again and I had a fresh set of distractions. In class, Peter had a crisp vitality, almost anger, in his tone as he rallied against money and the power of capitalism. He gave a lengthy speech on Ginsberg's "Moloch" and asked us to come up with our own examples. One kid, named Frank, objected. He looked a year or two older than the rest of us and he had bony wrists and an angular face. He said the class was turning into a Communist state and that Peter was a mouthpiece for Khrushchev. Peter snorted with laughter and drew a pyramid on the blackboard. He explained with a variety of arrows the dehumanizing impact of mass industrialization and homogenization, whether Soviet or American.

At the end of class, Peter seemed tired. His posture was stooped and his eyes were puffed and dark. "According to the Principal," he said, "I need to correct your homework. On the way out put your workbook on my desk."

As I waited in line, I noticed his big toes protruding through his moccasins. I wondered if he could afford new shoes, or even if he lived in Levittown.

"Workbook," he said.

"I'm sorry for what Frank said."

"It's O.K.," he said, collecting the workbooks from the students behind me. "People have a right to speak."

"But not to make accusations."

"Don't worry about it," he replied. "You should spend your energy on preparing for college. Did you hear any news on the scholarship?"

"Sorry," I said, hearing Frank's voice in the hallway, "I have to go."

Down the road I spotted Frank on the other side of the street, outside of an unfinished house. The base concrete slab was covered with snow and created a white platform one foot higher than the surrounding area. Peeking through the snow was a large pile of red roof shingles and another of two-by-fours. I picked up one of the planks and crossed the road to block his path.

He stared as though he didn't recognize me. "You're in my way," he said.

"Tolstoy was from Russia."

His mouth formed a thin-lipped smile, and he whipped his hands out of his jacket pockets to reveal brown woolen gloves holing in the palms. "You're that new kid. So, what do you want?"

Without thinking, I swung the two-by-four at his chin and grazed his jaw. Frank slumped to the ground in the shape of a snow angel. Dazed for a second, until his eyes cleared, he glared at the blood spots coloring the snow. I couldn't believe what I had done and I wanted to help him up and apologize, but I bolted home and spent the rest of the day in my bedroom.

* * *

After the fight with Frank, I used a new route to and from school. Not that I was scared of him. Fact was, I was embarrassed. The fight was a stupid move, and I had been full of anger. Taken my frustrations out on him. My life was not turning out the way I had always imagined. Growing up, my mother was a proud pacifist and told me violence was never the answer. Now I felt sick. I had let her down. I thought about my future as I took a shortcut to the edge of the neighborhood, trudging through the deep snow gathering in large drifts. Behind the community center was a new subdivision neatly apportioned into lots. Wooden posts marked where each house would be built. One post in the middle was leaning into the snow. I made my way to it and tried to maneuver it upright. The post was heavier than I assumed and it pulled me down. I got up and brushed snow off my jacket. The post had erupted out of its hole and I could see the remains of a potato plant, squashed and frozen.

At home, in the kitchen, Father was on his hands and knees sprinkling a white powder near the door. "We're being invaded," he said. "Ants."

"I thought you killed them."

"They came back."

"But it's winter."

"Sometimes God curses us," he said.

I went to my room and changed out of my damp clothes. When I returned to the kitchen, his head was in the cabinet under the sink. "There are ants in here," he said.

I didn't think it was strange he was obsessed with these ants; he was always fixated on one thing or another: pacing through the house switching off lights or reading through his files and memorizing his customers' names. I talked about the snow and how it wasn't really that cold outside. He grumbled an inaudible response, and I decided to broach the arguments offered in class and Peter's ideas about the power discrepancies in society. I detailed all the books we were reading, how he wouldn't understand.

He reversed out of the cabinet and sat on the floor. "Who is this Peter?"

"My English teacher."

"What's his last name?"

"Ritter."

"Why do you listen to him?"

"He knows everything."

"You should listen to me."

"Dad, you sell insurance."

He stood and slammed the ant powder on the sideboard. I thought he was going to raise his fist and strike me to the ground. He wobbled a little. "Listen," he said, taking my collar and tugging it for me to follow him. He went into his bedroom and opened the closet. He looked at me and then with his meaty arm swept aside the row of white shirts and gray suits. Above a shoe rack were shelves filled with the novels of Dos Passos and Fitzgerald and the poetry of Eliot and Pound. I could barely speak. I had been faintly aware of these authors, ones Peter had mentioned in class.

"Are these yours?" I said at last.

He nodded and picked up *Tender is the Night* and thumbed through the pages. He smiled when he noticed his own notes in the margin. "I bought this at a bookstore in Greenwich Village when I was first dating your mother. We used to read together in diners and coffee shops." He closed the book and tucked it under his arm. "Once we got married there was no time for luxuries. Other things were more important."

"Dad," I said, realizing I had to tell him now. "I'm heading to college in the fall."

Father was dumbstruck. His face momentarily paused as though he were plagued by neuralgia. "What about the job?" he said.

"I have one in a restaurant. I'll work there nights and weekends."

"You're not going to clean dishes and study these things." He held the book above his head. "What's important is a career that will give you a future."

"Mom wanted me to go to college."

"She said a lot of things. I wasn't honest with you before. She wasn't coming back."

"I don't believe you."

"I'm sorry," he said.

He leaned forward to try and hug me, but I stepped away and ran out of the house. It was cold, and, as I walked farther, I regretted not going back for my winter coat. Several times I tried to think where to go. I had explored most of the neighborhood, but in the dark it appeared alien—like a place I had never seen before. I thought of our old house in the city and my mother planting larkspur and coleus in her window box. She offered her palm for me to smell a handful of the wet earth...but now I could not recall the scent. Whatever Father said, I forgave her. I needed her memory. At the edge of town, I climbed a steep embankment and saw a painted sign that read: WELCOME TO LEVITTOWN. I huddled below the sign; my arms wrapped around my legs for warmth. Looking back at my route I scanned the tree line that faded in the middle distance, replaced by gray curving streets. I tried to make out my house, but I couldn't distinguish it from the rest.

* * *

Through the spring Father worked harder, spending up to fourteen hours a day selling insurance. He branched out to the more distant parts of the town, lengthening his walking route by miles. Each night he came home later and later. Something in him changed. He looked pale, almost sickly. In the weeks before graduation he collapsed in the road, a couple of streets over from the house. Neighbors carried him home and called a local doctor. When I saw him in bed, his body was thin and drenched in sweat and his hair ruffled. His skin was an odd shade of red, a blotchy maroon on his chest and in the hollows of his cheeks. The doctor told him he had suffered a heart attack and advised him to retire. "He needs bed rest and to be kept warm. Few distractions," he said to me in the hallway. I knew then I was responsible for him and the mortgage on the house. Father didn't say this was the case. But one way or another I had to care for him. I wanted to ask Peter about my college plans, but I found out from a classmate that he was gone. The Principal had asked him to leave. I heard later the school accused him of being a Communist after he mentioned Karl Marx repeatedly during class. There were rumors he found a job upstate or that he had gone back to California.

After a few weeks of sustained letter writing, the insurance company agreed I could take over Father's job. This was a mixed blessing at best. I was stuck here. Yet Father had quit drinking, for the most part, and now spent his days recuperating in his recliner. On my first day I experienced an early summer heat, a blistering warmth that felt heavy and damp. I took my jacket off, but my shirt stuck to the bumps of my spine. Even so, I felt more energized than I had in a long time and I walked for miles, weaving through the curved streets. New families were building houses and landscaping gardens with roll turf and rows of green saplings. Second-hand Buicks and Fords sat in unpaved drives, and young children playing Cops and Robbers shot me with finger guns. By the end of the day, I had managed one sale to a young couple who were interested in the death benefits of life insurance. I had tried to talk them out of it. I argued that the policy's advantages weren't that appropriate for them. They signed happily, though, and sent me on my way. I tramped home through the streets, then taking a shortcut through the yards, the wet grass staining my pant cuffs. I saw smoke rising from our chimneystack, and I entered the backyard and peered through the picture window. The living room was saturated in a golden-gray light. Standing by the fireplace, Father held an open book in his hand. I couldn't tell if he was reading the book or about to throw it onto the fire.

Summer Grass, Winter Worm

In his office, Cheng sipped his cup of *yartsa gunbu* tea and then rubbed his left shin, hoping the ache would soon fade. He took a second gulp, replaced the cup in its saucer, and rested his elbows on the desk so his hands joined, though not in prayer, but as a base to support his fat chin. He stared at the thin pile of crime reports—the list of petty grievances reaffirming his long-held resentment serving as the chief of police in such a provincial town. He longed for a post east in Chongqing, where he had a brother, or if the Party were smiling, Quanzhou.

Inspector Lin Shu knocked on the half-open door and came in. He was a stocky man, his chest easily filling the jacket of his olive-green uniform. His bony face was weather-beaten and his hands were rough from years in the fields. Cheng liked Lin Shu, who, as Tibetan, was trusted by the local farmers and yak herders.

"Outsiders struck in the fields again," said Lin Shu.

Cheng sighed. He knew from experience this matter would take some time to resolve. He rose from his chair, grabbed his cup, and went to the window that overlooked a sprawl of old *siheyuan* courtyards. "Last night?" he asked wearily.

"On the widow Yu's land."

"That will make things difficult." Yu was once married to Lungtok, a popular man who fought decades before against the invading Chinese army. He had died prior to Cheng's appointment in the town. A newspaper obituary reported his death had not been heroic—a simple heart attack one morning in the fields, while he was tending to his herd of yak. To counter the propaganda of the Party, the town whispered the legends of Lungtok's exploits. One, in particular, caught Cheng's attention. A baker in the square told him Lungtok had assisted the Dalai Lama out of the country by digging a tunnel from his house into the fields, to where his retinue spirited him to India.

"You will visit her today?"

Cheng nodded. "If my leg holds up."

"The tea helps?"

"A little," he said, looking at the cup's murky contents. *Yartsa gunbu* was the larvae of the ghost moth and was rumored to cure many ailments. He knew the moth laid its eggs in the grassy plains, leaving the hatched larvae to burrow into the dirt, vulnerable to infection by fungal spores. Over time the fungus subsumed the larvae, forcing a stroma to erupt out of the ground. The delicacy, known as worms, was harvested locally and sold to the dealers who came from Lanzhou and paid several hundred *yuan* for a fist-sized clump.

* * *

Cheng drove his old sedan into the square. He sped past the concrete statue of Chairman Mao and the shiny Zongshen motorcycles leaning against it and took the new asphalt road to the grassy hills that rose out of the plateau. The steep incline caused his engine to stutter as the road wound around the hills. He wished he owned a Land Cruiser, like his counterpart in Quanzhou, and he often regarded it as a slight that he had not been issued one. The road curved around the fields and ended in a giant loop that acted as a turning circle. He parked next to a wooden gate and climbed out of his car. The steep hill worried him. His leg had been tender for months now—a dull ache flared in the bone when he placed too much pressure on that side of his body. His doctor was unsure of the cause. Tests revealed little—although, Cheng was thankful bone cancer had been ruled out. In pain, he hiked the final *li* along a dirt path that curled around the hill and led to a large white farmhouse decorated with prayer flags.

A small boy opened the door and stared at Cheng. He sported a dollop of black hair cut in a bowl shape, and Cheng guessed the boy was around five-years-old. Before he could say a word the boy sprinted off, shouting several words Cheng couldn't make out. He stepped inside to try and talk to the boy again, to explain why he shouldn't be afraid. The house smelled of boiled duck fat, and Cheng heard the clang of cooking pots in the kitchen. Surveying the living room, he thought the furniture was in good shape—most of the farmers were herdsman and lived in yak-hair tents. Yu had done well. There were two *pegams* with hand-carved panels shaped in the lotus form and a row of silver-painted *thangka* boxes hemmed in by a sidewall. He peered through the small glass panels of a gold floral shrine and saw the shelves were empty of Buddha statues. A black-and-white photograph tacked above the shrine caught his eye. A man he assumed to be Longtok knelt on the hillside, grinning as he pointed to the vultures in the distance.

Yu appeared in the hallway. She had cragged pale skin and silver hair braided in a long ponytail. She wore a silk *chuba* and an amber bead necklace tight on her neck. Her eyes bunched as she studied Cheng and her hands began to shake. He tipped his cap, but she carried on shaking her hands, and he yanked his cap off and tucked it under his arm.

"*Tashi delek*," he said, offering his limited Tibetan.

"You're late," she noted, grazing past him and sitting down in a chair decorated with a coral-red temple. "Twelve hours ago would have been useful."

"I only—"

She pointed a bony finger to the picture of Lungtok. "Punctual man. He saved many lives."

"I heard," he said.

Yu snorted as though she didn't believe him. She went to the kitchen and returned with a wicker basket. She picked out a worm and held it in the air. "It took all morning to find this." She brushed the dirt off the larva and thrust it toward Cheng. The larva half was colored a dull yellow, while the fungus was dark brown and shaped like a thin twig. "But only this one."

Cheng pocketed the worm. "I will add a patrol for tonight."

"And tomorrow? And the next day?"

"Resources are limited."

She spat: "Those are the words of a politician."

The small boy popped his head around the corner and Cheng waved to him.

"Silang," Yu shouted, drawing the boy in. He stood next to Yu, hands behind his back, and lowered his eyes. The sleeves of Silang's woolen

89

chuba were frayed and speckled with mud. Yu spanked his rear and said, "Outside." Silang ran, crying.

Cheng hesitated to say anything. Lungtok had died at least eight or nine years ago and he wondered who Silang's father was.

Yu shook her head.

"Shall we go?" said Cheng.

Even though it was hot, Yu tied a brightly-colored *bangdian* around her waist and put on a white cloth hat. Cheng found it curious that she wore the apron, that she carried on the tradition as if she were still married. Yu led Cheng to her yard where a flock of chickens pecked in the dirt and some tools were kept in a ramshackle pile. She stuck a trowel in her sash and guided him to the fields. The sweep of green land stretched to the line of angular hills on the horizon. They walked toward them, and Yu shouted at Cheng to keep up. As she zigzagged through the long grass, she muttered he was slowing her down. "You need to fix that leg," she scoffed. "Fat man." She flipped the brim of her hat and knelt down to fer-ret in the grass for *yartsa gunbu*. She used the trowel to methodically part the blades and nestle into the earth. He knew the thin brown stalks grew barely an inch out of the soil and were difficult to spot. Although he had never farmed, his family had owned a sizable garden that sprawled from the rear of their house and grew pak choi and sorghum.

Yu moved on, searching another area with wildflowers sprouting in large clumps. Cheng caught up to her, and Yu cursed under her breath.

"Nothing," she said. "The men stole all the worms."

He studied the scene, hoping to find clear evidence this was the case. Although *yartsa gunbu* was valuable, it was also over-harvested. By uprooting all of the fungus, there were fewer spores to infect the larvae. He could not locate any freshly dug mounds and he crossed his arms, feeling defiant.

She glared at him and threw the trowel into the dirt near his feet. "This will be a bad season," she said.

Cheng could not disagree. The summer's end brought monsoons and a fusillade of extreme weather. Winter was nothing but sub-zero temperatures and cutting winds. He was not sure he could bear another one. "For all of us," he said.

Yu's brow creased, as if she were surprised by his forthright words.

"Send Lin Shu," she said. "He's a good man."

"Two policemen will come tonight," he replied, reaching for her trowel. He weighed the metal blade in his hand and then offered it to her. "They will be sufficient."

Returning to town, Cheng found a pilgrim truck parked on the edge of the square. Monks swaddled in vermillion robes were shifting small rolls of cloth off the bed of the truck. Over the years Cheng had witnessed an increase in monks passing through the town, selling rope incense and red clay burners to generate income for the monastery. Recently, the Party had passed a new tax penalizing the ground upon which a monastery was built. He wasn't sure how many months it would be until the monks began to protest in the streets and he would have to call in supplementary police from the other towns in the province. After locking his car, he followed the monks over to the market on the far side of the square. He jostled through the stalls, shaking hands with vendors who recognized him, and bought a bag of raisins. He ate them for a while until he noticed several men he had not seen before. They were crowded in a circle around a cardboard box filled with worms. The seller was a gold-toothed man who pointed to his hand smudged with numbers. The dealer wore a flashy red polo shirt and carried a cellphone. He laughed at the demands the seller was making and accused him of inserting lead wire into the worms to make them weigh more. Cheng sunk his hands in his pockets and walked away. The town had changed over the last few years, as the price of *yartsa gunbu* had sharply increased in value and brought outsiders in. Tired, he went home and telephoned Lin Shu, ordering a patrol to guard Yu's land.

* * *

Cheng woke late the next morning and arrived at his office without having eaten breakfast. He slunk in his chair, feeling flustered, and leafed through the fresh paperwork stacked on his desk. The report detailed a series of car thefts and traffic accidents and a stabbing at one of the bars flanking the square. "Drunks, no doubt," he said under his breath, and tossed the sheet of paper. He lifted his calf onto the desk and rolled up his pant leg so that his shin was exposed. Running his fingers over the fine black hairs, he searched for the cause of the pain. He could not find any external clue and he sighed.

Lin Shu entered the office carrying two cups of green tea. He plunked one cup on Cheng's desk and drank from his own. A little embarrassed, Cheng swept his leg to the floor.

"The widow Yu reported thieves again," said Lin Shu.

"She probably saw the policeman and mistook them for criminals."

"She's not happy," he said.

"I doubt she's ever been."

Lin Shu went to the window and checked his reflection in the glass. "You should have known her when Lungtok was alive," he said. "She was a different woman. Happy. Joyous."

"The past is a strange place."

Lin Shu smoothed down his jacket. "You're becoming a philosopher."

"I suppose."

"We were all yak herders then," said Lin Shu, turning to Cheng. "Yu fed us in the evenings: steaming hot *thenthuk* and a mound of flatbreads piled like rocks. It was a very different life."

Cheng could not quite picture Lin Shu's positive description of Yu. She had not offered him any hospitality—no noodle soup or freshly baked flatbread. He felt aggrieved in helping her. Yu, though, still had friends high up in the community and visiting her again would be the simplest of solutions. "I'll deal with her later," he said, and picked back up his paperwork. "Maybe this afternoon."

* * *

Cheng ate a late lunch of boiled mutton and greasy noodles and drank a large glass of dry *huangjiu*. He wiped the sweat from his brow with a napkin and felt the vibrating buzz of his cellphone. He did not recognize the number and he considered not answering the call.

"*Wei*?" he said, after a moment.

"Lijun," the voice said. "Ministry of the Interior."

Worried the call concerned a serious problem, Cheng remained quiet. It was unusual for the Ministry to bypass the National Police Agency—that much he was aware of. Then he remembered he had submitted a transfer request some time ago and he wondered if the Ministry was now reviewing it.

"Yes."

"The increase in crime. Unacceptable," said Lijun.

Cheng listened as Lijun listed the crime rates and berated him after detailing each one. Lijun emphasized that Cheng was shaming the Party and then he hung up.

Cheng flipped his phone onto the table, closed his eyes and deliberated on what to do. When he reopened them, he refilled his glass with wine and drained it in one swallow. He knew to be offered the transfer he had to lower the rates. Hazy reasoning led him to start with the theft statistics, and he drove to Yu's land slightly drunk and cursing his job. He parked his sedan at a crooked angle and slipped off his cap and rubbed his temples. A new slick of oily sweat coated his forehead and he wiped it away with his cuff. He thought of turning back, sending Lin Shu instead to deal with Yu. That would only make her madder, he sensed. He stepped out of the car and without shutting the door staggered toward the fields. Along the dirt path, he saw Silang running through the long summer grass. He noticed Cheng and bolted over.

"Hello," said Silang.

"Your mother at the house?"

Silang shook his head, lending a light flop to his mound of hair. "In the back fields," he said.

"You need a haircut," said Cheng, mussing the boy's locks.

Silang stepped to the side. "I want it longer," he snapped.

"All right," said Cheng, beguiled by the boy.

Together they walked to the farmhouse. Silang moved in bursts: fast and then slow—sometimes circling Cheng as if he were prey. "You're a strange one," he said to the boy. Silang reminded Cheng of his two nephews and how much he wanted to visit them again. His last trip to Chongqing had been almost ten months ago. When he returned he had conceded to himself how little he understood the land here and how desperate he was to leave.

Farther along the path, Cheng noticed a smooth shard of gray trapped between the slopes of the hills and realized it was a lake. As he focused on the contours of the shoreline—trying to remember the lake's name—he felt a cramp in his calf and asked to stop for a moment.

"Are you hurt?" asked Silang.

"No, it's just my leg."

Silang pointed to the hill. "My father is over there."

Cheng was confused. He shaded his eyes, but he could not see anyone. "Over there?"

"Would you like to see?"

Cheng half-nodded. He was in no hurry to talk to Yu again and he was curious to meet Silang's father. His leg was a concern. He reached inside his hip pocket for the vial of pills his doctor had given him. He swallowed two of the tiny orange ovals and gestured for Silang to lead the way.

"Follow me," said Silang.

Silang sprinted, and Cheng told him to slow down. Silang explained they needed to hurry, that the hills wouldn't be around forever. Cheng laughed and told Silang he was right, but that he was old. Silang stuck his fist out and his thumb up and said, "*Yapodu.*" Cheng liked the boy walking beside him and his constant neck craning to see if he was all right. He soon found, though, the steady incline of the hill deceptive and the air thin and his lungs aching a little. Then a strong breeze washed over his face and he could feel a rush of air inside of him. For a few strides he felt energized, like his old self. Then his leg twinged, the pain banding around the muscle as he climbed higher. He had doubts about what the doctor had told him, that he had been misdiagnosed. Cancer was infecting his leg.

Bending over, he rested his palms on his knees. He spat a glob of thick phlegm and watched the bloodied mucus weigh down a blade of grass. When he straightened up, Silang snatched his hand and tugged hard.

"You're strong," said Cheng.

"I know," said Silang.

Cheng allowed the boy to pull him up the last part of the slope. The grass thinned to patches of pale green and gave way to stumps of knotted juniper and finally an ash-gray moss. A sharp wind whipped Cheng's cap off and blew it over the top of the hill. Silang giggled and removed his left boot and threw it high into the air. As the wad of tanned yak leather fell flat to the ground, the pain radiated through Cheng's leg and he felt he was going to faint. He collapsed onto one knee and cursed himself under his breath.

"Are you all right?" asked Silang.

Cheng clasped his fingers around his shin. "Help me sit."

Silang guided Cheng to rest supine on the bare rock, and Cheng thanked him and looked at the brightness of the sky. A dusting of storm clouds massed on the horizon, and he thought of the long hike down the hill. The wind dropped away and Silang ran over to a small pile of rocks. For a short while, he watched the boy and how he kept his hands tight by his sides and his head lowered. When Silang didn't move, Cheng sat up and saw the rocks were actually bones. He had heard of sky burial: the ritual dissection of a body laid out on a flat slice of stone. Several vertebrae were missing and also both femurs. Wolves and vultures, he guessed, had gnawed on the body after the ritual cleaving of the corpse. Full of curiosity at this discovery he rose and hobbled over to Silang, to be sure what he was seeing. A dozen worms were arranged in a circle around Lungtok's sun-bleached remains.

"I remember him," said Silang.

Cheng knew that wasn't possible, that Lungtok was not Silang's father and had died before he was born. He put his arm around Silang. "We all remember him," he said, and held the boy tighter. As Silang knelt and touched the skull with his fingers, Cheng looked down to the fields below and saw Yu lugging a spade up the hill.

When You Find Us We Will Be Gone

On the sidewalk, the man picked up his begging bowl and counted the change. There were a dozen quarters, a couple of dimes, and a Canadian penny. He looked back at his sleeping patch, a narrow gap between a drugstore and a tattoo parlor. He had chosen the spot last night and marked his territory with a layer of newspaper. His once-blue blanket was a grubby gray and his canvas bag was stuffed with old correspondence. His makeshift bed stood a few feet from a dumpster. He had searched it earlier and found garbage bags filled with used bandages and hypodermic needles and then unearthed three soda cans, which he recycled at the drugstore.

Behind the dumpster, he rubbed saddle soap on his arms and face and rinsed it off with a bottle of mineral water. He dried himself with some of the newspaper from his bed. Using a fruit crate as a seat, he sat and read several of the letters from his bag. He drank dark navy rum. Every so often he hauled himself to his feet and peed against the sidewall of the tattoo parlor. He liked to make triangles and smiling faces. In the fading light, he smoked a cigarette and then lay down to sleep.

* * *

"Looks like a panhandler," said one boy to the other.

The two boys were identical twins.

"Let's see how much money he made," the second boy said.

The first boy nodded. "And if he resembles Father."

The twins walked past the dumpster and paused in front of the swollen blanket. The first boy picked up the begging bowl and poked the coins with his finger. "Three dollars," he said.

"A good amount," the second boy said.

97

The first boy slipped the change into his pocket and grabbed some gravel and dropped it in the bowl. He replaced the bowl carefully next to the canvas bag.

"Can you see his face?" the second boy said.

The first boy shook his head. He folded the blanket onto the man's chest.

The twins stood quietly for a moment.

"What's in his bag?" said the first boy.

The second boy took out the letters from the canvas bag. He read two of them. "Correspondence."

They examined a third letter together. They tried to understand what the words meant. "Symbols," they said. "They're all symbols."

The first boy searched for an address. "Where does he live?"

The second boy put the letter back with the others. "Here," he said. He turned in a circle, with his arms splayed wide.

The first boy laughed and copied his brother's gestures. He could smell urine on the wall of the tattoo parlor. He coughed and then coughed again to clear his throat. He crept over to the dumpster, got up on his tiptoes, and peered into the metal container. "It stinks," he said.

The second boy bent over the man and examined the ink stains on his face. "So does he."

* * *

The man woke to darkness. He reached for his Marlboros and shook one out. Lighting it, he saw the twins kicking the crate to one another. He noticed their sagging tube socks and worn sneakers.

"This is my patch," the man said. "Try across the street."

"We like it here," they said.

"I sleep *here*," the man said, and stubbed out his cigarette.

The first boy said, "It's a good spot."

"What do you want?" the man said.

The second boy said, "Can we sleep with you?"

"Are you cops?" the man said.

"We have money," the twins said.

"O.K.," the man said.

The first boy handed him the Canadian penny.

"Do you want change?" the man said.

The twins pulled woolen blankets from their knapsacks and settled the blankets to the left and right of the man's newspaper bed. The man brought out his bottle of rum. He took a swig and passed the bottle to the first boy. The boy sat down and drank.

"My turn," the second boy said.

A couple strolled past. Their faces were gray and fibrous. The woman carried a bag of groceries, and the man popped the lid of his pill vial. They crossed the street.

"Enough," said the man. He snatched the bottle and hid it in his jacket pocket.

"Bedtime?" said the twins.

"Bedtime," said the man.

The twins pushed off their shoes and positioned their knapsacks as pillows. Both of them hunkered down and rolled themselves inside their blankets.

"Comfy?" said the man.

"Comfy," said the twins.

All three gazed at the sky. The city light made it difficult to see the stars.

"Is that the Big Dipper?" said the first boy.

"Cassiopeia," said the man.

"Which is your favorite?" said the second boy.

"Gemini," said the man.

He lit another cigarette and looked at the twins. Left and right. Right and left. Their faces were round and smiling like the ones he peed onto the wall.

* * *

The man saw the morning traffic on the road. He rose and packed his blanket. "Time to leave," he said.

The twins shuffled about on the ground. The first boy rubbed his head. The second boy coughed. They stood and gathered their things. All three made their way to the sidewalk.

"It's early," said the first boy.

The second boy stretched his arms and yawned. "Any breakfast?" he said.

The man took out the Canadian penny and stuck it in the second boy's hand. "Here," he said, "spend it wisely."

"Do I get a penny?" said the first boy.

"You can split it," said the man.

The twins nodded and arranged themselves into a parallel position. In tandem, they approached the man.

"Goodbye," said the first boy.

"Goodbye," said the man.

"Goodbye," said the second boy.

"Goodbye," said the man.

The man put his begging bowl on the sidewalk and sat cross-legged behind it. He watched the twins walk down the street until he could not see them anymore.

Moonbow

When I moved into apartment 4E, a grimy one-bed walk-up on the Lower East Side, it wasn't for the view of the Coca-Cola billboard. It was more to do with Andrea, my wife. She was jealous of my time in the office selling overpriced home insurance. I was lousy at it and rarely made more than two or three sales a day. Cold-calling retirement villages in Florida, I would debate with the drunken supers the Gators' prospects and the fallibility of the BCS ratings. For hours we analyzed stats—receiving yards, sacks, interceptions—and then in the evenings I small-talked Omaha housewives, chatting about the tan leather sofas at Nebraska Furniture Mart and the new summer collection at Von Maur. After work I would take the subway back to the brownstone Andrea and I owned in Astoria, a block over from the East River. The year before, we had remodeled the kitchen after Andrea became obsessed with home improvement shows. To placate her I signed up for exorbitant loans to install tigerwood flooring and purchase high-end stainless steel appliances.

By the time I had lugged the oversized fridge-freezer into place, we had developed a strange arrangement of sharing the house. The master bedroom and en-suite bath were hers. I only possessed a temporary pass to brush my teeth and floss. The pine-panel study at the rear of the house, though, was mine. It offered a view of the communal garden, shared by the neighborhood residents. I could see the crescent pond dotted with yellow water lilies, the porch swing half-hidden in the shade of a ginkgo tree, and the beds of daises and roses overcome with wild, flowering hydrangea. At night, as the street light spilled through the study window, I sorted through my father's extensive collection of art prints and tried to rank them in an order he would have approved. Until his death three years ago he had assembled a portfolio of European work, including a fine Picasso lithograph, "The Youth Circle." The print was hand-signed in pencil and numbered 33/200. Jumping stick figures held hands and circled a peace dove. I kept the Picasso separate from the other prints and arranged them in chronological order, or in terms of market value, until I fell asleep in my Barcalounger and started the cataloging again the next day.

When I saw my wife, our once sweet talk was reduced to an awkward system of qualifiers: "maybe," "perhaps," and often, "I have to check my work schedule." Andrea worked for an advertising agency and was taking extension classes in PR and Marketing at Columbia. She berated me for not keeping our dinner plans, or attending the theater with her friends, or visiting her parents. Andrea came from a wealthy family in Westchester. Her mother and father drove matching his-and-hers Mercedes C-Class sedans to the country club, where they played tennis with potbellied pros, and enjoyed post-game cocktails in the bar, gossiping about who could use the lake house in the Adirondacks.

This state of affairs lasted until Andrea changed the brownstone's locks. For an hour I stood on the steps and tried to reason with her. She would only communicate through the intercom: "Robert, I can't do this anymore." She sobbed and continued in a weary tone, chastising my passive attitude to life and the nauseating happy-go-lucky stance to our relationship. A bout of silence was punctuated by a loud crackle and thud, as if she had punched the intercom panel. "Why don't you have a better job?" she screamed. For her, this was the crux of our relationship. She was embarrassed by my lowly job title and incensed by my refusal to apply for a promotion. The issue followed us into the bedroom, as the last time we'd had sex was months before when she wanted kids and I said I would think about it.

I was an insensitive jerk, for sure. But I was young—well, spiraling into my thirties—and ready to move on. Our relationship was done. In a coffee shop, near the brownstone, I studied the classifieds in *The Pennysaver*. One ad described a rent-controlled walk-up near the J Line. I met the landlord in the tenement's lobby. He was a rotund man, who liked to have an unlit cigar in his mouth, and spoke in short pulses. "Sure thing," he repeated several times, as we agreed on the lease. He fidgeted with my business card, passing it from hand to hand, and directed me away from checking out the neighborhood, particularly the abandoned garment warehouse opposite. I liked the old redbrick building and the large billboard on the flanking wall that faced the apartment. The advertisement seemed to have been replaced countless times, as its rips and holes revealed the same faded image underneath: a 1950s-style full Coca-Cola glass with *Zing!* emerging from the bubbles.

There was one room: a combined bedroom and kitchen with a plasterboard alcove that turned out to be the bathroom. For privacy, a thin yellow sheet hung down from a curtain rail. "Open plan," the landlord called the place. Lack of plan, I thought. I rented the apartment anyway and signed a twelve-month contract. I envisaged this as a chance to revisit my bachelor days, even back to my years at Haverford. I slept on a cot borrowed from a friend and bought microwavable hamburgers and burritos from the deli on the corner. After my shift I would buy a fifth of bourbon from the liquor store and collapse into my recliner, the air-conditioning on full to dry my sweat and block the sound of traffic outside. When the TV worked, the weatherman whined about the late summer heat wave and the dust particulate coming in from the West. When it didn't work, I took walks through the neighborhood to Hamilton Fish Park and thought long on how I was going to improve my situation. I would circle the large swimming pool, taking several minutes to complete one loop. I felt sorrier for myself than the destitute boys who swam in their tattered boxer shorts and the homeless men who slept on the benches.

Although the park didn't have the same ramshackle beauty as the garden, it started to be a place I would visit on the weekends. I settled cross-legged on the tight-cut grass and watched couples and families jostle in and spread holing floor rugs and neon-pink beach towels for picnics and sunbathing. There was something idyllic about the sunlight glancing off the tan bodies and the secret bottles of wine shared in bright red Dixie cups. The intimate conversations and playful touches to the arm and knee reminded me of my first dates with Andrea, when we both lived upstate and took long drives out to Belmont Lake to hike in the woods and have sex by the shore. We would drink rich porter beer from squat bottles. She could rarely handle her third beer and would become a mean drunk, complaining that I was a lousy lover. Now watching these couples left me sick, forcing me to look away and run back to my apartment for a tall glass of something cold and alcoholic.

It was after one of these trips to the park when I first heard my neighbor. His words were barely discernible, just a faint echo through the cheap brickwork that separated our apartments. He had a strange tone, broad and choppy, as though his voice box were generating noise through a blender. I listened at the wall, but he gassed out his monologues in a far section of his apartment. Via a series of experiments, I learned that if I opened my window and squatted on the inner ledge, I could make out his words. That night there was a rant about the city's tax system. He especially liked to repeat, "They're always screwing us working stiffs." On other nights he was eloquent and learned, giving recitations of Shakespearean soliloquies. The strange emphases he put on Hamlet's "To die, to sleep" and "To grunt and sweat under a weary life" were unnatural, often leading me to turn up the TV. However, it was his quieter moments, his murmuring in relation to meteorological phenomena, which caught my interest. At length, he would read out long tables of atmospheric pressure and then link the high altitude results to a word I had never heard of: moonbows.

The word intrigued me, and when my wife shipped my possessions across town, it was my childhood encyclopedia that I first dug out from under my shredded suits. The short entry read: *Moonbow: A lunar rainbow. See Rainbow (lunar).* Unfortunately the R section was damaged, torn and stained a dark pink from a two-decade ago Kool-Aid accident. Still, my imagination filled in the gaps, a speculation that moonlight formed the rainbow. My neighbor spoke on this topic regularly, around two or three times a week. "Purity," he said one day. "A line to God," he said on another. The evening he mentioned God, I was sifting through the packing crates for my father's art print collection. As he continued his lengthy description of the perfect moonbow, I scribbled notes on the brightness of the Moon, my position relative to the Moon (I needed it behind me), the optimal rain conditions, and the darkness of the sky. According to my understanding the darkness was, of course, the biggest problem. The lights in the city were far too bright to see this phenomenon. Even if I switched the apartment lights off and decreased the glow of the city by a magnitude of ten, there would be still no chance I could see one. I thought a great deal about a solution. Somehow I would need to have a complete absence of all artificial light. Any practical way of achieving this was beyond my liberal arts education, and for a while I gave up on ever seeing a moonbow.

Soon after this low point the divorce proceedings began, and I fell into a habit of smoking before bed. I would perch on the window ledge, half in, half out. I wasn't afraid of the drop, as the ground below suggested at least one answer. I didn't want to die, but I was bored with my new existence. Now that my wife was out of my life—and my father's passing had fully hit home—I had few people to speak to. Even the calls at work were losing their charm. My neighbor's speeches offered a modicum of respite and I came to depend on them for intellectual stimulation. Once, when I leaned quite far out, I caught a fleeting glimpse of him. He was a pale man, older than me by at least twenty years, his hair graying at the temples and his scalp badly balding. He was sitting on a low-level chair next to his window, his face vacant. I edged into the apartment—unsure whether he had seen me—and smoked two more cigarettes before I dared look out again. He was still there; this time he did see me. His eyes bore into me as if he was frightened, and he rolled backward in what I could now see was a wheelchair.

I felt guilty, but not so guilty that I immediately went around apologizing. If I waited a day or two it would give me an air of nonchalance, an indication to him that I hadn't been spying, that it had all been a great misunderstanding. As the weeks passed, the impulse to visit him left me. I enjoyed listening to him too much. He was like a disembodied spirit trapped in another world. I even pushed my bed closer to the wall so I could doze with his voice drifting into my head.

* * *

The previous occupant of my apartment must have been a foreigner. Or, at least, a connoisseur of the more ephemeral manifestations of world culture. He left a bamboo box stuffed with rooibos tea and a carton of dried buckwheat in the kitchen cabinets. Behind the hot water heater, I found a Day-Glo poster of Bob Marley glued to a thick sheet of Plexiglass. I couldn't tell by the mail sent to the place which of the old tenants fit with these odds and ends. I counted six or seven names and in conglomeration they were receiving credit card offers and personal finance assistance, back issues of *The Nation*, *Dog Fancy*, *Cigar Aficionado*, and *Hot Rod*, Tibetan and Pakistani food menus, and postcards from Sapporo,

105

Johannesburg, Toulouse, and the Marshall Islands. The most worrisome letters were from a debt collection agency and were addressed to a Japanese-sounding name: Mr. Ashikaga. Though the owed amount was only seven-hundred dollars, I resolved to ask my neighbor if he knew much about this man.

One Sunday afternoon, sometime later, I caught sight of my neighbor on the trek home from the park. At his open window, he was studying the Coca-Cola billboard and the two workmen replacing the neon tubes that framed the advertisement. He wore a black sweater vest with a military-green button-down shirt underneath, and in a stiff movement he leaned forward, his hands gripping the sides of the frame as though he were in pain. From my limited angle, it was difficult to tell what was going through his mind. I attempted a half-wave, but wussed out and ran my hand through my hair. He saw me and glided away into the darkness of his apartment.

In the evening, I enjoyed a couple of drinks as I argued with my wife on the phone. She wanted me to sign over the brownstone to her in exchange for the Picasso and the rest of the collection. I told her I was busy and she should talk to my lawyer. She hung up, and I grabbed two beers from my fridge and stepped into the hallway to speak to the neighbor. With the first knock, my weeks-earlier plan of nonchalance went to hell. I knocked too lightly and so on the second attempt I over-compensated, banging hard on the door like a madman locked away in a Victorian asylum. Within seconds, I heard the metallic squeak of his wheels.

"Who is it?" he said.

I leaned close to the door, swearing that I could hear his gentle breathing on the other side. "It's your neighbor."

"What do you want?"

This question stumped me. *What did I want? What was I doing here? Why didn't I stay in my apartment and drink a third bourbon on the rocks?* I wanted to hoof it out of there, retreat to my recliner and *Sunday Night Football*. I almost convinced myself that he wouldn't notice, that he would blame it on kids, weak-willed social services, or immigrants.

"It's your neighbor, Robert. Robert Black," I found myself saying.

"And?"

"I want to ask you about Mr. Ashikaga."

The door opened slightly to reveal his sallow gray face and a pair of bifocals nesting in the loose strands of hair slathered over his scalp. Creased lines around his eyes exaggerated the slight bump on his nose, and he had one of those glares that seemed impervious to human interaction. I bent down and presented him a beer through the two-inch gap.

He brought down his glasses to study the bottle of Bud Light. "I don't touch the stuff," he said. "So, who are you?"

"As I said, I'm your neighbor. I've been meaning to come around the last couple of weeks. But you know, with work and all."

He snorted and coughed up a ball of phlegm. He spit it into a pocket handkerchief, probably monogrammed with his initials. He seemed to be the sort. After a short pause he unhooked the chain, and I entered with the smile I used to give Andrea, a kind of upended grimace.

His apartment had two bedrooms and a clean kitchen that opened up into a spacious living room, organized so he could easily move around it. Against the wall, stacks of shoe boxes were labeled in a regimented manner: Newspapers (1980-85), Newspapers (1986-1990), Letters (Martha), Letters (Mother), State Maps (no Alaska or Hawaii), State Maps (Alaska and Hawaii), Certificates (Achievements), Certificates (Government and State), Weather Reports (National), Weather Reports (Local). Yet for all the room's efficiency the decor was unfashionable, as if the place hadn't been redecorated in years. The burnt orange wallpaper was festooned with snaking roses, and the coffee table was lacquered with black varnish like it was straight out of nineteen-eighties Japan. Well-thumbed periodicals *The Meteorological Magazine, Weather Chasers, Storms Monthly* were fanned on top.

"Nice, huh?"

I peered down at him. His wheelchair was similar to the ones I had seen at St. Luke's. Black nylon seat and backrest, powder-coated steel frame, thin rubber tires. It was all a little depressing.

"Great," I replied.

Expertly he gripped his handrims, pushed forward, and rolled to the window. He braked over two shaded grooves in the linoleum, where I could tell he sat day after day. On the nightstand were camouflage-patterned binoculars, a heavy-duty aluminum flashlight, the remains of a Swiss cheese and Genoa salami sandwich, and a cup flecked with dried coffee. It was clear he spent a lot of time alone, and I felt a pang of regret that I hadn't come around sooner.

I drew up a stool so we were the same height. "I'm Robert."

"I know," he said, crossing his arms. "John."

"I'm sorry about seeing you at the window. I like to smoke on the ledge and—"

"Do you have a spare?"

"Yeah, sure." I passed him the pack along with my lighter.

"It's been years since I had one of these." John lit the cigarette, bent forward, arm resting on the ledge, and smoked. He coughed a little as he inhaled several deep drags, holding the smoke in longer than I had ever done. He carried on talking, as if his small indulgence had never happened. "What do you want to know about Mr. Ashikaga?"

"I'm not sure. He left rather a lot of stuff behind. I guess I'm trying to contact him. Do you have a forwarding address?"

"No," he said. "Check with the landlord."

"Right."

"He was a Jap. An Asian. We didn't have much to say to each other."

I wiped the beer from my lips. "I'll ask the landlord."

"So," he said, looking me up and down, "I guess I should ask what you do."

"I sell home insurance."

"Sounds like a waste."

"It has its moments."

John made a strange noise, a sort of lengthened huff. "Army man myself," he said. "Cartographer with the Corps of Engineers."

"Really?" I said. "Interesting work?"

"We created military maps," he said, his chafed hands drawing an imaginary square. "I used reconnaissance photographs, local intel, and available data to draw enemy installations, roads, and airfields, onto a master copy. At the Pusan Perimeter—that's in Korea by the way—General Walker commended my work. It got me promoted twice by the end of my service."

He didn't look at me as he spoke—only at the view outside, which was similar to mine. I conjectured that he could see a trivial degree more of the park. I was a little jealous of the section of dry grass, the late sun on the pool, and the geriatric grandmothers with hair arranged like loblolly pines, walking their Mal-Shi and Bichon Frise, oblivious to anyone else.

"They supplied us with free Coke during the war," he continued. "Rotted half my damn teeth." He opened his mouth wide to reveal blackened molars and a missing incisor. "Spent years trying to find a good dentist."

"How long have you lived here?" I asked, trying to divert the conversation away from his poor dental hygiene.

"Since I retired," he said, picking up his binoculars. He peered through them, out to a spot in the distance. "Perhaps too long," he added, after a while.

"I know what you mean. I'm not sure I fit into this neighborhood."

"Think you're too good?"

"It's not that." I finished the second of my beers and rose to leave. He waved me down, revealing the striated muscle of his arms and the creep of blue spider veins.

"My wife died three years ago," he said, resting the binoculars in his lap. "We had been living in this neighborhood for fifteen or so years, something close to that. She was the one who kept track of these things."

I wanted to tell him that he was lucky, that women—despite their benefits—were no good. Instead, I nodded and asked him what had happened.

"It was in the news. 'Death on FDR,' they called it. Funny how I remember the headline. I don't feel bad telling you the details. God knows, I've bored Mrs. Powell enough with them. One morning Martha and I were out for a drive. In fact, heading to Trenton. Martha had family there. Just as we reached the intersection a Hummer clipped our car, and she crashed into the barrier. She got a steel pole in her head. I was left with this." He gestured to his thin legs, which were hidden beneath his elasticated pants.

I should have told him I was sorry, that I was a jerk for asking, and that it would be good if I left. I said nothing and listened to the rest of the story. He survived on his veteran benefits and a paltry sum from the insurance settlement. That money bought him an aide, Mrs. Powell, who delivered a cold sandwich lunch, helped tidy the apartment, and wheeled him once a month to the Catholic church a block away for Sunday Mass. He didn't strike me as particularly religious. He displayed only one cross in the apartment, above his boxes, probably nailed there by Mrs. Powell or an old neighbor. But there was an ever-present conviction in the stories he shared with me, an evangelical passion for the life he used to lead.

* * *

Our friendship developed its own routine. I would stop by after work to check on John, bring him a pack of Camels, and talk about our respective days. He would sit near the window dressed in khakis and a polo shirt, the buttons done up to his neck. Sometimes he wore dark pants and a dress shirt, the shirttails untucked or his laces undone. I wondered about the practicalities of how he got changed, how much Mrs. Powell did for him. He was always clean shaven. Once, he let me use his bathroom and I saw his lowered toilet and sink and his swivel-mounted mirror. I wasn't sure what he thought of my stubble, as I barely shaved. When it came time to listen to his long lectures, I settled in with a large tumbler of bourbon. He talked for hours on a single subject: the best method to fire-cure the dark leaves of Kentucky tobacco; the money-wasting of the EPA; the complicated plays of his high school football team. It turned out we both loved the Jets, though we differed on our opinions on Woody Johnson. John supported the guy in all of his decisions, even his politics, and argued he was one step away from being holy. I didn't care for Woody's conservative leanings—and I said so—but that didn't stop John poking fun at my support for universal healthcare and free education. I didn't tell him that I went to Haverford on a scholarship. For sure he would have said taxpayers paid for my education and worse—even worse than Andrea saying it—that I never achieved anything afterward. When he talked about *his* wife, which was usually to reinforce how the neighborhood had gone downhill once she died, I asked questions. But in truth, he barely paid much interest to my inquiries.

Almost by accident I found out his last name was Wallinger. One day, while thumbing through my mail in the lobby, I glimpsed his apartment number. The mailbox originally read MR. & MRS. JOHN WALLINGER, but an unknown party had used a Sharpie to scrawl over the neat handwriting, leaving a big J.W.

Apart from the handful of conversations we had about his wife, he rarely referred to anything personal. Once or twice I mentioned my wife, her paranoia, or at least her way of legally receiving a quick divorce. Andrea was claiming adultery, naming one of my co-workers, who was older than my mother and had a penchant for Sudoku and chamomile tea, as my lover. John would refuse to process these talks. Rather, he would focus the attention on the weather patterns he would observe through the seasons: blizzards, Nor'easters, electrical storms, tinder dry air currents, wet downbursts, and most often, nimbostratus and cumulonimbus, commonly known as rain clouds. He created his own classification of the latter, based upon visibility and the amount of water that would pool on the sidewalk. His terms ranged from "a panhandler's spit" to "Biblical flood." He kept the results in a wide-ruled composition notebook, often drawing elaborate line charts and circling the days and times of unstable weather.

In a moment of openness, one late evening, he recalled he loved night rain the most as it was the greatest chance to see a moonbow.

"Have you ever seen one?" I asked him.

"Not yet," he replied. "The conditions here are against it. You would have to go Hawaii, or New Zealand, or even one of the National Parks out West. I've seen pictures. They're beautiful, usually a white curve low in the sky." He rotated his upper body to his boxes and opened one labeled Moon (Light). He exerted a great deal of energy sorting through the pile of official-looking documents, newspaper clippings, and typed-up notes. "Here we go," he said, passing over a small photograph.

The black-and-white landscape had darkish-gray mountains and the outline of a pine forest. A waterfall burst from glacial granite and an arc of brilliant white crossed the water. Captured moonlight. Frozen in time. It reminded me of the art collection that I might not see again. I tried to describe the Picasso to John, mentioning how the lithograph was inspired by his desire for world peace.

"Never had much time for his silly paintings," he snapped.

John's attitude drew me back to my own when I was a child. My father hung the piece in his study, above his desk, and shot it admiring glances while he leafed through the newspaper. For decades he worked in

111

a cannery, before retiring weak with diabetes. He spent his retirement fixing up the house and entertaining me when I came home from school. I thought the pictures were a waste of money.

"We should plan a trip," I said, holding up the photograph.

He wheeled over to the window and yanked the cord of the blinds, the slats zipping down in a deafening clatter. "I can't leave here."

"We can work past your disability."

"My disability has nothing to do with it." His eyes locked onto the photograph of him and his wife that hung on the bedroom door. "Martha didn't like the outdoors. She hated bugs. Anything that bit her gave her a rash."

"At least she wasn't a parasite, like mine," I said. Andrea had dropped the adultery allegations and hired a private detective to search through my financial affairs for more material she could use. John seemed irked. So I carried on talking, hoping to recover the situation. "If we leave the city, you'll get a chance to see a moonbow. Maybe she would have wanted that."

"You don't know anything."

"When was the last time you went outside?"

He snatched the picture from my hand. "Get out," he said.

"Come on, John," I said, my tolerance fading. "Don't you miss talking to people, grabbing a bite, betting at the track, confessing to the priest?"

"Get the hell out of my house."

I didn't push the issue for a week or so. I wanted John to go with my plan. We both had nothing to lose, and I hadn't been on a trip since my fifth wedding anniversary. Yet however much I put it to him that we could leave the city and head out West to see one, he refused, citing everything from the congestion on Broadway to the late arrival of his morning newspaper. I could tell he didn't want to talk about the real reason, about the death of his wife. At night, when I was in bed, I could hear him shuffling papers and moving to his window, the familiar sound of a lighter clicking and him smoking. I imagined, as he peered out, that he would remember his wife and the life he used to enjoy.

* * *

At some point that is slightly hazy to me now, I met John's aide in the hallway. She was older than John, possibly an impression caused by her thinning silver hair and ugly beige cardigan. Clutched to her chest was a torn pocketbook stuffed with coupons for Pedigree Good Bites. She introduced herself as Mrs. Powell.

"Are you the new neighbor?" she asked.

"That's right."

She scrutinized my bare feet and appeared baffled by my lack of socks and shoes. "He talks about you," she said. "All the time."

Her words took me by surprise. It was strange to think of John enjoying my company, taking solace in the things we talked about. I wasn't sure if she was jealous or just relaying the information. "Ditto," I mumbled, conscious of the fact I should have something more significant to add.

"You're younger than the last tenant."

"Mr. Ashikaga?"

"No, he hasn't lived here for years. Mr. Ok..."

"Okoduwa?" I said, remembering a brightly-colored postcard from Lagos.

"Sounds right," she said. "I'm glad I got to talk to you. I'm worried about John. He hasn't been to Mass for several weeks and his health..." She lowered her eyes and searched her pocketbook. "His smoking doesn't help."

Feeling guilty, as I held the cigarettes for John behind my back, I said: "I'll talk to him about it."

She passed me a Mass schedule and hobbled over to the stairwell. She held the rail as she struggled down the stairs. I regretted that I had judged her, that I was still acting like a jerk.

"Do you need any help?"

"I'm fine," she said and kept going.

Before I knew it I had her arm pressing on my shoulder, using me to aid her balance down the two flights. She talked of her son Gregory, who resembled me, and lived across the country in Seattle. He worked in finance, specifically microfinance, helping women in Bangladesh with accessing small loans for clothes repair businesses. She even gave me his card and said if I ever wanted to change careers to give him a call.

113

Once I had walked Mrs. Powell to her car, I let myself into John's apartment with the spare key he had given me for the cigarette runs. Inside, he was reorganizing his stack of boxes by writing new labels for a new top layer focused on natural disasters. He had already penned Earthquakes (Northern Hemisphere), Earthquakes (Southern Hemisphere), Tidal Waves (Asian), and Nuclear Fallout (Military), and he held six more labels that were blank. As he wrote on the next one, his hand went into spasm and his Sharpie fell to the floor.

"Mrs. Powell might be onto your smoking," I said, picking the pen up and handing it to him.

"She worries about me," he said, sticking Global Warming (Hoax) on the box. "Some days she reminds me of Martha."

"She does seem nice."

"Not bad," he said.

I brandished the schedule. "This is for you."

He glared at the thin slip of cardstock. "You hold onto it," he said. "I don't need it so much anymore." From the Manila folder on his lap, he picked out a thin wad of newspaper articles, paperclipped in the upper left-hand corner. "I wanted you to see these. I've been collecting data on sea level decreases. But you'll never read about it in *The New York Times*."

I examined the yellowing slithers of paper and found them to be written in German or Dutch. "I can't read these."

"They say Antarctica is actually *growing* in size."

"I'm pretty sure the icecaps are melting."

He snatched the clippings back and stuck them and the folder in the box on the coffee table. "It's a con," he said, "a liberal attempt to raise taxes on the sly for welfare." He rolled to the nightstand to pick up his binoculars and angle them toward the park. I was confused by his logic, but followed him over. We saw a drab-yellow school bus pull up near the entrance and a group of Down syndrome kids and their parents exit the bus and shuffle into the park.

"We should go, too."

"Because I'm disabled, right? There's nothing wrong with my mind."

"John, come on, that's not what I mean. I thought the park would be a change. We can get a breath of fresh air."

"I get that from the window."

"You're being ridiculous," I said, sounding like my father.

He threw the binoculars hard. My head flipped back in surprise, but somehow after they whacked my sternum I caught one of the lens barrels. A blossoming soreness banded through my torso, and I rubbed my chest. His face flushed. I handed the binoculars back.

"I'm sorry," he said. "I didn't mean to do that."

"It's my fault," I apologized.

"Leaving is not a good idea."

"If you ever want to go, we can use the maintenance elevator."

"Robert, I'm not a trash can."

This was one of the few times he addressed me by my name. I wasn't sure what it signified. Perhaps it was a moment of direct connection—that he understood how we came to be in the same room, how we came to be friends. I held up the pack of Camels. "You can have these if you come with me." I witnessed the weakness in his face: he kneaded his temples and twisted the gray tufts above his ears. "We'll be back soon and then you can sit here and rant. You can throw things at me all you want."

I pushed his wheelchair to the park. He resisted at first, but within fifty yards he tired himself out and said he was taking a nap. He was lighter than I thought, barely ninety pounds, and he was so slight that I imagined his loafers would slip from the bone stumps of his feet. As we passed through the gates, he raised his hand for us to stop. His thin fingers curled into a ball as he took in the grass lawns and the line of birch that led to the pool. Perhaps, like me, he could smell the tree pollen and the chlorinated water, scents rekindling after-school trips with my father.

"Take me around," he said.

We circled the pool languidly, his wheelchair gliding over the smooth concrete edge. The water was colored a kind of odd translucent blue that captured the sunlight and kept it trapped at the pool's bottom. Gentle waves lapped against the curb. Amber leaves, small knobby twigs, and struggling black flies rode the crests. In the shallow end, the kids from the bus were in pumpkin-orange life jackets, splashing and laughing.

"My wife is dating a new man," I said, as we completed one loop. "Her private detective."

"Women died in Pusan. Civilian casualties, they called them."

I wasn't sure if he was trying to cheer me up or if he was just recalling the war. "Did you see this happen?"

"My maps got them incinerated."

I stopped pushing and reached for the flask inside my jacket. Without thanking me, he took a long, hard swallow and kept the flask clasped in his lap. The talk of his military work riled him and appeared to have drawn him back to his past. I wanted to quote Montaigne or Proust, or offer a profound aphorism of my own, reassure John that he wasn't responsible for anyone's death. For whatever reason I had nothing and I sat down on the baking hot concrete, and together we watched the sun set over the water.

* * *

I didn't see John for a couple of days. I had a sales conference in Poughkeepsie, training fresh recruits from the local community college how to sweet-talk Florida's pensioners. When I returned to the city, I had to deal with my wife. We finalized the sale of the art collection. She kept the proceeds from all the prints, except the Picasso. That was mine. I promised her in the upcoming weeks we could talk about finalizing the divorce or enroll in marriage counseling, if she wanted. She agreed, and following a few glasses of wine, she let me sleep on the couch.

The next day after work, I enjoyed a drink with my colleagues and I told them about my wife and our issues. Pints of beer and a vodka shot or two later led to an extended monologue about John and his obsession. I described moonbows, but most assumed I had invented them. Almost as a joke, my boss suggested that I should secretly organize a trip and then strong-arm John into it. I said I would, and on the way home I stopped at Port Authority to buy two Greyhound tickets to Yosemite. With boyhood glee I kept fingering the ticket envelope in my pocket and thought of the possibilities that awaited us. I imagined a deserted spot beyond the camping grounds and the hordes of tourists, near one of the remote hanging valley waterfalls, water shimmering out of the granite. We would be far away from John's memories and my wife. At night we could sit and wait for the rain. Wait for the arc to form.

Through the streets to my building, a wet wind carried the smell of pretzels and the wail of far-off sirens. At the tenement I was still half-delirious and bolted up the stairs two at a time. When I reached my floor, I sensed something was amiss. John's front door was open and on his coffee table a map was spilling out from one of his boxes. He was close to the window, leaning forward in his wheelchair. The curve of his back highlighted the grime of his Barbour jacket and the medals pinned to his chest. He didn't turn when he heard me come in. So I joined him to see what he was looking at.

"John?" I said.

His hands were pressed against the sill, and he was staring at the billboard.

"John, are you all right?"

"Look at it, Robert," he said softly, "look at it."

The Persistence of Vision

It occurs that there is
sometimes an image not the same;
but what before was woman, now at hand
is seen to stand there, altered into new woman;
or other vision, other age takes over;
but sleep and oblivion coalesce
that we shall feel no wonder at the thing.
                    —Lucretius
                         trans. Edward Lawrence (1922)

Memory, as with conscious thought and perhaps even unconscious thought, originates from our perception and then repression of the world. In close proximity to this formulation emerges a new theory: the persistence of vision. Within the connections between the eye and the brain sequential images, which through time form memories, replace one another in a steady progression. The mind—a superior grade of camera—remembers, stores, and positions these images. But to what end?
                    —T.K. Maylor, *Principia Optica* (1908)

Sometime later, it occurred to me that the mail had arrived on a Sunday. This had never happened in the years I had lived in the neighborhood, a section of Brooklyn often referred to as *up-and-coming* and *respectable* in realtors' jargon. The two-bedroom apartment I shared with my wife and daughter overlooked the street, a thoroughfare only busy in the early morning and in the late afternoon when hundreds of commuters retreated from work. On that particular evening in April, a rainstorm had passed an hour or so before and left the pin oaks outside wet and glossy, marooning a smell in the air so strong that I closed the bathroom window. The smell was difficult to describe, and in my profession that is a problem. Eventually I settled on *fresh peat mixed with Virginian chewing tobacco.*

I stared at my typewriter, an Olivetti I had bought at a pawnshop on the Lower East Side. I wrote a page of Proust-inspired prose: a stream-of-consciousness re-telling of the rain and the smell, two events connected by my obsession with detail. I leaned back, vaguely disappointed with my writing. The framed antique map on the far wall caught my eye. The map—doubtless a modern copy—was gray and faded. At one time it had shown a Mercator projection of the world: a bulging Greenland, an omnipresent Antarctica, an engorged Europe. I had always opined the map looked slightly off, as though the original had been drawn from memory.

Below the map was my daughter's violin, upright in its stand, and my wife's area—a solid-looking Windsor chair next to a plain escritoire—where she crocheted doilies, potholders, and dishcloths. Sarah had always been strait-laced. Even at her bachelorette party she had refused to drink or dance, leaving the restaurant early to go to bed. My daughter, Mary, was much the same; toys and games were of no interest. Although she was eight, she preferred to read Jane Austen and Emily Brontë and spend hours practicing her violin. As I thought of my wife and daughter they emerged from the bedroom, prettily attired in matching white sundresses, for a piano recital at Lincoln Center.

Sarah came over to where I was sitting. "You're not ready."

"I have work to do," I said, gesturing to a stack of paper.

"We were supposed to attend as a family."

"I need to finish this section."

"But you promised you would go."

I shook my head and fed a new sheet of paper into the platen.

Sarah went back to Mary and whispered in her ear. "Daddy," I thought, was mentioned several times. I stood and walked past them.

"Where are you going?" she said, calling after me.

"The mail."

I took the stairs to the lobby, a part of the building in some need of renovation. The walls were lined with wooden panels and had scrollwork near the ceiling that curled into a series of pillars, ten feet apart and crudely shaped in the ionic style. At the base of each were rubber plants housed in white alabaster pots. Occasionally, a fine air swept through and gently rustled dust from the leaves. The mailboxes were situated in an anteroom at the lobby's rear. In a moment of kitsch, or possibly desperation, we had relabeled our box MR. & MRS. JONATHON LUMEN. A move that had since paid no dividends for our relationship. Inside my box I found menus from a Chinese restaurant, coupons for a discount grocery store, and a letter addressed to David Phot, the protagonist of my first novel *Here is the Light*. I rechecked the envelope to make sure I had not misread it. In my book I had set up Phot, a middle-aged man, to lose his wife and daughter all for the misremembrance of another woman. The cause was unclear. He was a psychiatric-optometrist, a self-invented field that connected conditions and variances of the eye to episodes of abnormal behavior. Before I wrote the novel I had read one of Freud's early works, the *Psychopathology of Everyday Life*, and I integrated his notion that error in everyday life is triggered by memory repression: a deliberate substitution of the false for the true.

Through the door's frosted glass panel I saw blurred versions of Sarah and Mary leave, and I turned my attention again to the letter. My publisher was re-releasing the novel in a special edition and they thanked Phot for his permission, attaching an advance for seven-thousand dollars.

121

I couldn't understand why the check was made out to Phot, and why he was receiving the money. For a split second I doubted that I had been the novel's author, that somehow my fictional Phot had written his own story. I read the letter again to make sure that it was not a practical joke, some sort of hoax that would be elaborated later on in the tabloids or on cable television.

There was a strange requirement for the dated check to be cashed. The letter noted how Phot was scheduled in a week to read from the novel at Second Ink, a used bookstore in the East Village. Without the reading, the check would be canceled. I had visited the store once before: a year or so ago I had been looking for a first edition of Edward Lawrence's *In Hope We Find This Nation*. His book—of which I had glimpsed only a fragment, a loose sectional translation of Lucretius' *De rerum natura*—was part of the research I was doing for an abandoned novel on false pattern recognition in the city's history. The store didn't have a copy. The owner, in fact, refused to look up the title on his system. "There's no such book," he said. I tried to reason with him. I mentioned the monographs, academic papers, and personal journals it had been referenced in. I summarized, as best I could, Lawrence's obsession with binaries, his theory of dialectics, and his explanation of capital. He had a notion that everything was controlled by a powerful company named Allmen Inc. "I would have heard of such a book," the owner finally noted.

At my apartment, with the letter in hand, I went immediately to the telephone so I could call the bookstore to check that the event was real. Something stopped me, a feeling that perhaps it was a case of intellectual revenge by the bookstore owner, or just a simple mistake by the publisher, or even that it was my agent supplying a late April Fools' joke. I carefully placed the letter next to the telephone and brewed a pot of coffee as I ogled the brownstone across the street. I had lived in Park Slope for many years; the meager square footage of the apartment evidence of my meager book sales. Yet the brownstone always seemed like it should have been my home: a three-story building with plenty of room for an elaborate study and personal library. The man who lived there resembled me in several ways. He had a similar build: a thin, lanky body of six-foot-two, salt-and-pepper hair, and an obtuse nose that could be described as Roman. My neighbor also worked unconventional hours; he usually slept in his

Barcalounger during the day, a newspaper on his lap, a cup of coffee on his side table. The biggest difference between us was that he lived alone. I had never seen a woman or anyone else in the brownstone. It seemed like a path I could have taken, a perennial bachelor or a loner unwilling to sustain personal relationships.

He stared directly at me, and I considered waving or even pretending I didn't see him. I placed the cup on the sill, stretched my arms, and settled down in my own recliner. My level was equal to the windowsill and it would be difficult for the man to observe me further. I hoped he wouldn't think of me as a voyeur or pervert; I was neither. Although I was sure we had made eye contact in the past, it had always been glossed over as a momentary lapse, a stalemate between the two of us.

* * *

After a light dinner—a simple feta salad, laced with Arbequina olive oil and the last of my Pohnpei pepper—I left the apartment with the letter, anxious to avoid my wife and daughter before they returned home from the recital. I had decided not to involve them, as they were innocent of any involvement in the letter's provenance.

I caught the 4 train to Manhattan and exited at Union Square, close to a café I frequented in graduate school. A ten-minute walk toward Greenwich Village led to the circular brick-and-glass building of Second Ink. It was a one-story construction, shaped like a Friesian paper mill. The long glass slots were mirrored and spaced evenly around the outer wall. Unsure of the store's connection to the letter, I approached with caution. A young woman was inside the doorway arranging the bargain books. She had a Russian dictionary tucked under her right arm, carefully positioned next to her tan cardigan. The way the cardigan complemented her skinny black jeans, eggshell white blouse buttoned to the top, and cork-heeled sandals reminded me of a girl from my childhood. I couldn't picture the girl's name or exactly where she existed in my past. She could have been the girl next door when my family lived in Ames, Iowa, or the girl I escorted to high school prom a decade later.

As I got closer, she heaved the books down. I became self-conscious; my heavy stubble and crumpled clothes made me feel like a turn-of-the-century bindlestiff. Even so, I considered going in and explaining to her who I was and how many books I had sold. Though that would not have been impressive. Showing her a copy of my novel, the fine grain of the paper and the exquisite stitching into the spine, would intrigue her more. Perhaps the hardcover would be slyly shown to her in a fit of modesty, over black tea and crumbly coffee cake, with me ably fulfilling the role of humble writer. Then the author photograph on the inner flap: magnanimous proof of who I was and who had written that dense story centered on a strange and obsessive man in New York.

The woman fiddled around for something in her pockets. I reared back, frightened that she had recognized me. Though I wanted to speak to her, to discover our connection, I knew now was not the correct time. I crossed the street and pretended to examine an antique nightstand in a store window. Then I marched two blocks to a newsstand and bought a pack of Lucky Strikes. I smoked a couple as I browsed the magazines: feigning interest in TV listings, current news events, and celebrity pregnancies. The country outside of the city rarely interested me. My life existed within narrow confines, and this gave me boundaries for each day. My needs were met: food from the organic co-op on Union Street; shelter in my apartment; companionship with my wife; love from my daughter. The last two were lies, falsehoods promulgated by our living situation. A fact none of us wished to recognize.

On my return to the apartment Mary was in bed, her body snug in candy-striped pajamas. Sarah was kneeling next to the box-spring, her graying blond hair tied in a topknot. She draped the comforter over Mary. Mary yawned. She had the same face as her mother and the hair she used to have twenty years ago. I imagined at that moment Sarah was smiling, and I plucked a cigarette from my pack and searched my pockets for a light.

"Good night?" she said.

"I went for a walk."

"I thought so." She turned back to Mary and stroked her hair.

"How was the recital?"

"It was Liszt-heavy: 'Valse oubliée,' 'Mephisto Waltz,' etc."

I slipped the cigarette in my mouth. " 'Waltz No. 2' ?"

"No." She studied me before lowering her eyes. "Will you go to the window?"

In the living room, I exchanged my cigarettes for the letter. The envelope was a regular 4x6 with a stamp in the right-hand corner, but no postmark or return address. The letter itself had been typed on a cream-colored bond paper. On the signature line were the initials P.D. followed by the embossed logo of Corona Press, a black circle faded at the perimeter. I sat down and considered what P.D. stood for. The letters were the reverse of Phot's initials. Perhaps this coincidence was part of the joke. It could also have been shorthand for Police Detective or Private Dick. I held the check up to the light. The color and feel of the paper appeared to be genuine. Everything, the name, the address, all felt correct. For a long while I held the letter as I gazed out of the window, watching the tumbling pageant of cirrus clouds glow in the light from Manhattan.

* * *

The next morning I awoke to find Sarah had gone to work. For the last three years she had taught in an elementary school in the neighborhood, a job she had taken once Mary had begun kindergarten.

I consumed breakfast naked. At the kitchen table, I picked at a bowl of oatmeal topped with thinly sliced banana. My gangly torso had a potbelly. On the left side I had a scraggly appendectomy scar that ran a clear three inches. I could still feel the remains of the stitches, small craggy lumps of tissue. I had been born with *situs inversus*, a genetic condition that reversed the placement of my organs. During my first examination, the doctors discovered my heart on the right-hand side. Any negative effects, they said to my parents, could be mitigated by a sedentary life. In my mind growing up, I had no other choice but to become a writer.

By midday, I arrived at the conclusion that I had to call Vollis Pilarski—my agent of seven years. We had met at a writers' conference in Vermont, a ten-day affair of workshops, readings, and networking. Vollis only conducted fast conversations. He would deflect questions with a "Let's move on" or "We'll schedule that for our next meeting." On the conference's first day he had signed me, securing a two-book deal with Corona a few months later. On the rare occasion I called the office, I often talked with one of the agency's secretaries. Two were named Caitlyn, one spelled with a K. A fact she had insisted on in my last call. A third woman,

Rachel or Raquel, never recognized my voice. In that day's conversation she took my details, pronounced my surname *Loo-man* as if I were a washroom attendant, and after a long pause transferred me to Vollis.

"Did you send me a letter?"

"Any chance you can be more specific?" he said. "There's always mail going out of the office."

"A funny letter, like a joke."

"I don't have time for jokes."

I could hear a strange buzzing sound in the background, as though the phone were bugged or someone were recording the call. "What's that noise?"

"Listen, I've got to go," Vollis snapped. "Call me when you get the book finished."

For over two years I had shelved multiple drafts of my latest novel and—in the process—discarded a legion of meta-fictional ideas, crotchety characters, and labyrinthine plots. I didn't regard it as a case of writer's block, but rather writer's choice. The options of creation were too varied and large in scope for me to narrow down what the new book should be about. The reviews of my first novel were uniformly negative. *The New York Review of Books* highlighted the poor (and misogynistic) character- ization of women. The *Washington Post* agreed but went further, railing against the ludicrous plot and the ambiguous ending. Several critics noted a certain pretension in the writing, a cryptic obsession with encyclopedic facts and obsolescent words. Poor sales followed, and the novel's failure had left me hollow—a creeping despondency that had increased over the years. The book was rarely in the stores anymore and my copies at home were locked in the safe.

The phone clicked.

On replacing the receiver, I saw the neighbor across the street in his study talking on his phone. His face was red and his mouth showed some teeth as he shouted. This was the first time I had seen any emotion in him. It was an odd feeling. My double had a darker side, an unstable center that was rarely seen. Perhaps that was why he was alone, why he avoided people and social contact. Stooped down, I crept into the lounge and positioned myself by the bookcase. From this angle I had a reasonably clear view of his actions. His call was over and he was now at his desk, searching the drawers, pulling out papers and files and a slender lockbox, which he unlocked with a combination. The contents—a black notebook— he immediately hid in his jacket pocket. He rose from his chair and left the room, perhaps to leave his apartment.

In my youth I fantasized about becoming a hard-boiled detective, tracking down criminals and chasing leads. Now this was my chance. The relative closeness of the neighbor's brownstone meant my best option to shadow him was to complete a loop from my building to the subway station. The route hooked me past a row of boutique stores and the Vespasian. In the restaurant, a young and tanned waiter with gelled hair and a slim build was setting the outside tables for dinner. In a careful and precise manner he positioned the salad plates, brought out the breadbaskets dressed with gingham cloths, polished the wine glasses with his napkin and laid the cutlery in military fashion, a set for each course.

When my neighbor traipsed past muttering to himself, I turned to pursue him. He had an uneasy walk: a kind of fast step, using his shoulders to aid forward motion. I stayed twenty or so feet behind him. He crossed the street and circled the block to end up on Prospect Park West. He kept to the edge of the park, occasionally looking in at the sweep of oak and maple. At the northwest corner, he slipped through the entrance and stayed with the path for half a mile. In the heart of the park he sat on a ribbed metal bench, where he had a view of the baseball diamonds and a collection of residential buildings beyond. He jotted something in his notebook. I imagined he picked out vivid details of the softball team playing in the distance: the muscular legs of the batter, the third baseman chatting on his cellphone, the grass stains on the buttocks of the umpire's uniform.

The man went to the cinderblock restroom not far away, and I took his seat on the bench. On a scrap of paper from my pocket I tried to recreate what he had written. I closed my eyes. Teenagers scampered through the outfield and over to the lake, laying perpendicular at the water's edge and looking at the gray water and the fighting white swans. The ballplayers carried on with their game, grunting and wheezing through the inning. Only when the teenagers disappeared from my mind did I think of my neighbor. He had not come out of the restroom. I ran around the building to find an exit on the other side. I felt foolish. He was probably at his brownstone, as I would be, listening to Luigi Cherubini's "Les Deux Journees" or reading the black and blank pages of my favorite Laurence Sterne novel. I decided not to return home.

* * *

Gray clouds massed on the horizon and by noon filled the sky. I remembered the woman on the radio had mentioned a storm. Outside Union Square, to which I had traveled again, a homeless man was setting up an umbrella stand. In his cylindrical plastic pot, which resembled a quiver, he had three rainbow-patterned golf umbrellas. In a scarcely audible voice he repeated the same words over and over: "Eight dollars. Eight dollars. Eight dollars." He reminded me of a minor character from my novel, an aging playwright who roamed the streets, treating the entire city as his stage, the residents as his actors. Out of pity I bought an umbrella and walked briskly to the bookstore.

Taped to the front window of Second Ink was a large sign for the reading. There was no author photograph, just the novel's title and the words: A SPECIAL EVENING WITH DAVID PHOT. The curve of the glass distorted my profile, pushing my features away from each other. I could barely make myself out. I was a blur, a person in two states at once: both Jonathon Lumen and someone else, someone that I was unsure of. At the counter in the store was the young woman from last night. Her tied-back hair had the remains of an auburn colorant, and her body was thin and supple. She had fair skin and keenly muscled arms that rarely struggled with the heavier books. She hauled one pile to the floor then started to arrange the items near the register. On one side were art house postcards featuring grotesque portraits and infra-red landscapes and on the other were pencils embossed with writers' names: Voltaire, Whitman, Poe. For an unexplained reason the latter was formatted P.O.E., as if the writer were an acronym for three other words.

I slid the pencil out from the clear plastic holder and tapped it on the counter in an uneven rhythm.

The woman glanced up from the pile of postcards she was counting. "Can I help you?"

"Strange pencil," I said, unsure if she recognized me from last night.

"That's one of our biggest sellers."

"Because of the style?" I asked, holding it up.

She gawked at the pencil, as though it were the first time she had seen it. "I've never noticed that before. Must be a printing error, I guess."

I pointed the pencil at the sign in the window. "Do you know much about next week's reading?"

"Only what's written on the poster. But hold on." Her brow creased a little as she opened up a large planner and thumbed through its pages. "It only says that David Phot is reading from his novel at eight o'clock." Her finger traced over the sentence a second time.

I wondered again about the owner that had acted strangely a year ago. Perhaps out of spite he had orchestrated the whole thing. "Are you selling the book?"

She pointed to the large stack near the entrance.

I went over and picked up a copy. The cover was the same: the blurred shadow of a man silhouetted by a bright white light. Phot's name was on the front. Everything was identical as the first printing, except for the name. I pivoted back to the woman. "What's going on?"

"I don't understand."

I held the novel up so she could clearly see the cover. "I'm the author of this book."

"Are you David Phot?"

"Someone has taken my book and changed the name."

She didn't reply at first; she seemed to be figuring things out. "I'm sorry, we booked David Phot. Look, his name is on the jacket."

"He's my creation."

She raised her eyebrows in a way that I wasn't sure if it were in empathy or fear. Maybe she wasn't involved with the deception, maybe she just sold books. I backed off and asked where I could get a good cup of coffee.

"Try the place on 12th," she said.

I bought the book without waiting for the change. In the light rain, I carried it under my jacket—tucked tightly to hide Phot's name. The café was the same one I used as a base during my study for a psychology degree at NYU. The inside had changed in the last fifteen years. There used to be grungy school desks and chairs, and baristas with heavy black eyeliner who quoted Schopenhauer. That had all gone, replaced by sleek round tables with hard granite tops. I ordered an espresso and found a table at the rear so I could view everyone who entered. For some reason I couldn't admit to myself, I hoped the woman would stop in once her shift finished. She offered something Sarah couldn't: a fragment of a lost past, an image of an alternate life. It was strange then that I was concerned she mistook me for Phot, that she had seen another man inside of me, a double from whom I wanted to escape.

I opened the book and searched for an author photograph or biography. The jacket flap had neither. Both had been replaced by white squares. As I rifled through the pages I saw the story had been remixed into a continuous string of random letters, a pattern that occasionally produced phrases like "findme" and "intothedarkness." If this were a hoax, it was an elaborate one: a lot of money and effort had been spent on tricking me. If, though, Phot were a real man who had taken on the name, then I needed to find out who he was. It occurred to me that he sat among the patrons. A couple of men could have been candidates: one table removed, a man around my age was reading the *Washington Post*. He paged through the newspaper to the crossword puzzle, and I heard him mutter the clues and his answers as he filled in the blank squares. Invariably they were the wrong answers. For "Southeast Asian country" he wrote *Lout*, and instead of writing *T.K. Maylor* for another, he had squeezed in *P.T. Barnum*. I almost tapped him on his shoulder to dictate the corrections. It would have given me a perverse fillip if I had done so. On leaving the coffee shop, I slapped the man's puzzle. "Ten down. The answer's *Capitalism*," I said. "Not *Confucianism*." He gave me a startled look then folded his newspaper in half so I couldn't see the crossword. "It's none of your business," he said and shooed me away.

In the doorway, I bumped into the woman from the bookstore. She gave me a brief smile that was almost a look of pleasure, an indication she had similar feelings of longing and familiarity. I mumbled, "Excuse me," and hoped she would follow me outside.

"Hey," she said, calling after me. "Are you enjoying the book?"

I let two suited men pass before I spoke. "I'm having trouble getting into it."

"I'm sorry," she replied, her forefinger touching her lower lip. "We have other novels in the store. Nabokov. Borges. Auster."

I ignored her sophomoric suggestions and said: "I'll stick with this one."

"All right, let me know how it works out."

"I've read it before, but I've forgotten how it ends. I'm sure I'm repressing a memory or two," I said, ending my statement with a noise that was half-laughter, half-grunt.

"That sounds Freudian."

"Would you like to go for a walk?"

* * *

We walked for miles; past a steak house that smelled of French fries and beef gravy; past Rockefeller Center, where she commented on the architecture; past the Russian Tea Room, where I remembered an afternoon spent with my wife; past Columbus Circle, where we looped the roundabout twice. For a short while, we discussed Freud. She knew little beyond jokes about cigars and slips of the tongue. She smiled when I told her I had authored a dozen papers on him. "And a book, too," she added, laughing. She still didn't buy my confession that I had written the novel. I told her about my medical condition and she felt for my heartbeat, laughing again when she found it. "Maybe you did write that book," she said afterward.

I explained to her that Freud surmised misspoken or unintended words were caused by past trauma repressed by the mind. For years, in Vienna, he had studied human speech patterns and tried to ascertain the meaning of people's mistakes. In the prime of his career he had examined this phenomenon in literature, studying the Bible, Shakespeare's plays, the poems he sent to his mistress. The woman clasped her hands together as if to pray and said she used to write poetry in high school, love sonnets that she later burned. She looked sad for a moment. On a whim I quoted a line from one of Donne's *Meditations*—"Still when we return to that *Meditation*, that *Man* is a *World*, we find new *discoveries*"—but claimed the words as my own.

In Central Park, we huddled together underneath my umbrella, our bodies close and her hand occasionally touching mine. The rain poured down around us. We left the path, skipping over puddles, the mud and grass soaking our shoes. She commented upon my suit, said it was "Handsome, like a matinee star's from an old black-and-white film." Circling a softball field, we heard the sound of children's laughter. We saw the twinkling lights of a carousel and the horses resplendent in bright red and green saddles. The rain had slackened, and a group of adults were drinking chardonnay and watching the carousel spin and spin. They ate birthday cake and lined up to go on.

"I thought it would be closed by now," she said.

"Would you like a ride?"

"I'm not sure we're allowed."

I bartered with the owner, a grisly man with pocked beige skin, to interrupt the private party. I gave him the last of my money, fifty dollars in tens, and we sneaked on around the back. We sat on two horses—one behind the other. As the carousel started, I held the pole and strained my neck to keep her in my sights. She, in turn, looked at everything. She absorbed the lights, the music, the return of the childish screams. My breath shortened, my mind rippling with elation. Time distorted into a swirling mass, as if I had always been riding the wooden horse and she had always been close.

Once the ride was over, we left the park in silence and ambled for a few blocks farther. As we passed a run-down hotel, I asked her if she wanted to go inside. She snatched my hand and led me into the lobby. As a joke, we booked a room under the name Mr. & Mrs. David Phot. She laughed when she read it in the register and smiled like the girl from my past, the one who always seemed nameless and just out of reach.

The room was sparsely furnished. The queen sported floral sheets and the nightstand was rickety, like the one I had seen in the antique store. A cracked hopper window let in a ripe breeze, diluting the smell of Lysol from the bathroom. We both lay on the bed and looked at the dimpled ceiling and the bare light bulb. I flicked the switch and undressed, sucking my stomach in the best I could. She hiked up her skirt and pulled me in. Our limbs crossed and uncrossed, finding the odd nooks of flesh satisfactory, and she slid on top, grinding me and speaking words that I could not understand. Once I had ejaculated, neither of us spoke for the longest time. She faced the nightstand, and I turned to the view of the building opposite.

Eventually I spoke. "I have to get home."

"Where do you live?"

"Park Slope, with my wife." The words came out without fore-thought, drawing a look of disgust on her face, as though she had seen me soil myself.

"You're married?" She looked at my left hand. "Where's your ring?"

"We have an agreement not to wear them."

"I'm not sure I believe you."

"If it weren't for my daughter, I would have left years ago."

Tears welled in her eyes and she wound the sheet around her chest. "You should go."

I dressed hastily, stuffing my socks and underwear in my jacket pockets. At the door, I asked for her name.

"Please leave," she said, and rolled onto her side. Her body contorted into a malformed S—her thin and muscular limbs rigid and angular, a pillow tight to her chest.

As I sprinted through the lobby, the concierge grinned at my early check-out. I almost returned and hit him for his impudence, for his knowledge that she had paid for the room, that things had not worked out between the woman and me. However, it was late and I needed to be home.

* * *

In the apartment, I could hear a voice and the sound of the violin. For several minutes I listened in the hallway. Eventually I recognized the composition as part of Vivaldi's *L'Estro Armonico*, a dark and somber section that often caused me to wonder about the piece's formulation. I followed the music into the lounge where Sarah sat at her escritoire, crocheting a winter scarf. She gave instructions to Mary in a grave tone: "Détaché," she said. "Détaché."

Beneath Mary's eyes her skin was puffy and shaded a dark purple.

"Shouldn't she be in bed?" I said.

"We were timing how long you would be." Sarah motioned to Mary to put down her bow. "How many concertos you would miss."

"I don't think that's important."

133

"You never do." She threw down her crochet hook and examined me more closely. "You're soaked," she said.

I pushed back my hair and pictured my umbrella tossed at the foot of the hotel bed. "Caught in the storm."

"It barely rained around here."

"It was a long walk."

She moved to where Mary was sitting and caressed her shoulder. "Let's go," she said, guiding Mary out of the room. "We'll talk about this later."

That night I stripped off my suit—the pants and jacket hung over the shower rail—and I settled down on the recliner. I lay quiet and still, unable to sleep. I spent my time looking at the brownstone, its lights extinguished. I imagined he was in there, hiding from me, perhaps seated at the far end of his study watching, writing his observations in his black notebook. Maybe he found out I had tailed him and was exacting his revenge. His disappearance in the park left me interested as to his fate, for I had not seen him since that day. It was possible he had split from the city and relocated to another town, or state, or emigrated abroad to locate his ancestry. My mind swirled with possibilities, unable to shut down. As the night wore on I tried a host of remedies: I drank a mouthful of chamomile tea then threw the cup in the trash. I completed a deep breathing exercise that endowed me with strange energy and I read for hours, rereading the same page over and over.

* * *

In the days that followed, I returned to the bookstore on several occasions. A male college student, who confused Homer with Virgil and Thackeray with Dickens, seemingly replaced the woman. She might have run away with the neighbor, I speculated, both of them living at the run-down hotel, planning their future together. There was no doubt that she had gone with him to the Ukraine, or the Balkans, or from wherever his family originated.

On one visit I saw the owner. He was dressed in the same navy blue slacks and black turtleneck I had seen him in a year earlier. His short gray hair was neatly combed to the right side and he had an aggravated cough, as though he smoked too much. I waited to see if the student would show up for his shift so I could ask him about her. The store had a circular design, with the register in the middle and the shelves flexing outward as radii. This meant I browsed one side then the other, turning at the ends. I sorted through obscure histories of the Hudson River and the annals of New York property law, searching through indices for a mention of Edward Lawrence or *In Hope We Find This Nation*. Although that project was behind me, part of its essence lingered within. Out of a perverse habit my body succumbed to this obsession, a type of muscle memory that drove me to hunt in every bookstore or dig through familial effluvia at each junk sale I came across. Yet, in the end, I knew the owner was my only option.

"I'm looking for the girl who works here."

He coughed into his fist. "Who are you?" he said.

"That doesn't matter. I want to know how I can contact her."

"You seem familiar."

"I talked to you a year ago about a book I needed for my research."

"I don't remember."

"My name's Jonathon Lumen."

"Is that supposed to mean something?"

"Listen, just give me her number."

"This is a place of books, not numbers," he said, wafting one hand in the air. "Look around. Over there's history. Behind you and to the left, social sciences. Near the door, illegitimate novels."

As I followed his arrogant gesticulations, I realized this man was controlling recent events. "You're the one who's been screwing with me," I said. "Sending me letters, creating fake books. What do you want? What are you after?"

"Sir, you're mistaken," he replied, his posture stiffening. "If this is about her, this woman—whoever she is—then I suggest you contact the police."

We both stood in silence. It was possible he knew nothing of what I was saying. I imagined he was trying to place me, figuring out the precise details of our previous meeting. He was sweating, especially the fat of his neck above his collar. I could tell he wanted me to give her up. There was something about her—intelligence, humility, vulnerability—which I desired. It was more than physical, though there was still a trace of her perfume on me. It was her mind that I wanted. She had been talkative on our walk, although her exact words had faded.

I scribbled my number on the blank side of a postcard. "If she comes in, give her this."

He snatched the postcard and slung it in the register.

* * *

That night I barely dreamed. A fitful sleep punctuated with images of dark spaces, wide and eternal. I roused several times, thinking I had heard the phone. On each occasion, I leaned over and touched her body. The skin felt fleshy and warm. Womb-like and repugnant. By early morning, I found myself staring at the ceiling and recalling the intricate decay of the hotel room's stucco. In the darkness, I dressed quickly in yesterday's clothes.

Before Sarah woke, I slipped out of the apartment to retrace my route. I looked for the woman first in the café, where office workers had taken over all the tables. In the phase before work, the men and women were staring at their cups and writing to-do lists on napkins. My inquiry to the barista resulted in a stern reply. "Hundreds of women come in here every day," he said and looked to the man behind me. Following this dismissal, I visited the steak house. It was closed and not due to open for hours. Shivering a little in the cold morning air, I questioned how much she had understood and how much she had even listened. Our talk of Freud had been superficial, fragmentary. The understanding we had existed only for a short time, a brief burst of magic where the rules of normal life—if there were such a thing—had not applied. Was it too much to want this for a lifetime? The question caused a pang in my stomach and near Rockefeller Center, it hit me again as I tried to envision what she had said about the building. The words briefly fell into place: *Art Deco design* or the *golden ratio*, but I wasn't sure.

Seeing the Russian Tea Room, I recalled again the date with Sarah. Years ago, just before Mary was born, the afternoon had been cold and an ice storm was due that night. We had settled down at a table with a pot of Earl Grey and a plate of English muffins spread thickly with butter. We talked for a long time about nothing in particular. In a momentary lull she asked a stranger, an elderly man reading a newspaper seated at the table next to us, to take our photograph. We stood close together. My blue suit and her blue maternity dress signaling us both as compatible in our marriage. A certain reticence, though, existed that meant neither of us put our arm around the other. The final image caught two figures barely smiling, both with the thought that the love had gone.

At Columbus Circle, I barely mustered the energy to search for the woman. The traffic was in gridlock; an accident down the block was responsible for the disruption. I headed into the park, glad for the open space. I moved on at a slow pace, trying to retrace our steps. My legs felt heavy and stiff and my sense of direction dissolved on the curving paths that swept through the grassy meadows and hidden groves of maple and pear. As sunlight flared through the wispy clouds, the carousel became visible a hundred yards off. The building was boarded up and a handwritten sign read: CLOSED FOR REPAIRS. Bright red Dixie cups and soiled napkins gently swirled in the breeze. I peered through the shutters at the horses. They were still and dark.

I exited the park dejected. I had failed to find her and I was unsure where she had gone or if she would return. Whoever this woman was, I needed her. The reading was in the evening and there was a chance she might attend. Then it came to me. If I showed up with my copies of the book, I could prove I wrote it.

* * *

In the dim hallway, I could hear my daughter in her room singing "Ring-a-Round a Rosie," something I had not heard her perform for years. She emphasized *we all fall down* by slumping to the floor. Again and again I heard the crunch of her slight body hitting the parquet. Each time she sang the nursery rhyme she got louder, as if it were a magical incantation. I almost went in to rejoice in the spectacle, but Sarah entered Mary's room and shushed her.

The living room was subdued in an ethereal blue light; I felt like a shadow as I went over to the map. Behind it was the safe, where I kept my financial documents and my copies of *Here is the Light*. The situation mirrored the Schrödinger's cat paradox: the books existed both with my name and Phot's at the same time. If I didn't look at the books, it meant the possibility existed that they had the name Jonathon Lumen on them. There was a chance I was not paranoid or delusional, but simply the patsy in someone else's plan. I lifted up the map's wooden frame and held it as I examined the safe. The numbers on the dial were in intervals of ten—from zero to one hundred. The longer I stared at the digits, the less sure I became about who I was and what I was doing. I replaced the map at the sound of footsteps.

"I think it's time we talked," said Sarah. She had red marks around her eyes, as though she had been crying for several hours.

"Not now."

"I've hardly seen you in days. What have you been doing?"

"Have there been any calls?"

"Calls? What do you mean?"

"I don't have time for this," I said. "I have to be at a reading."

"This has to stop."

"You don't understand." She grabbed my arm and held it with a firm grip. "I need a father for Mary...I want my husband back."

"Leave me alone."

She let my arm go and observed me as I headed for the bathroom. I swallowed three of her pills with a little water and then, without checking to see if she were still watching, left the apartment.

* * *

At the 7th Avenue station, I nipped into a crowded car full of young women dressed for a night partying in Midtown. Most wore denim skirts, thin white vests that revealed braless chests, and they clutched in their hands large, sparkly pocketbooks. Men lingered close by, looking on, half-remembering past dates and ex-lovers. When the train stopped at Bergen Street, I saw on the platform two women who barely acknowledged the opening of the doors. Their faces were grim and an unnatural shade of yellow. From their pocketbooks they dug out index cards with the letters P and D printed upon them. These women, these letters. It all seemed too much to be a coincidence. Someone was using me for his or her own fancy. I looked away, closing my eyes until we left the station.

Exiting Union Square, I wandered in a daze to the bookstore. It was a long, staggered journey that took double the regular amount of time. My head swam and my legs felt bruised. The room was arranged with forty empty seats and a desk stacked with copies of *Here is the Light*. I went inside, curious as to where everyone was. I caught a whiff of aged Virginia tobacco, and I could hear applause, a steady clap getting louder and louder. It was an uneven and grainy sound, as though the same clap were being repeated at different intervals. Copies of copies of copies. On the desk, to the side of the books, was a cassette player. I could see a tape playing. I inched back, unsure of what was going on. I heard a muffled voice from behind the mirror at the far end of the store and saw the edge of something black. The owner stepped out and paced toward me. He grabbed my hand and shook it brutally.

"Mr. Phot," he said.

"No, that's not me."

"Mr. Phot," he said again.

"Don't you recognize me from yesterday?"

"Yes, you're David Phot. The writer."

"Why do you say that?"

"You're here for the reading."

"I don't understand."

"Everything is set up as you specified."

"Listen, I don't know what you're talking about."

"Please come this way," he said, as if he had not heard my answer.

We walked between the chairs to a wooden lectern. I could hardly process the owner's motives. Imaginably to him I was Phot. Maybe he had met him before and misinterpreted our meeting, conflating the two of us as one. The owner gave a mild bow to the empty chairs and gestured for me to come forward. I stood behind the lectern and gripped both sides of it. My eyes shifted from the small pitcher of water to the spotlight above me. I felt a change inside, some force trying to escape. I drew the novel from my jacket and opened it up. In my clearest voice, I began to read.

Here is the Light

In treating the pathological-obsessive, or some variation thereof, it is necessary for the practitioner to divide his mind: one half interlocutor, the other instigator. I am told Sigmund Freud found this method to be of the greatest use.
—Sir Charles Frampton, *Methodologica* (1928)

I leaned back, vaguely disappointed with my writing. The framed antique map on the far wall caught my eye. The map—doubtless a modern copy—was gray and faded. At one time it had shown a Mercator projection of the world: a bulging Greenland, an omnipresent Antarctica, an engorged Europe. I had always opined the map looked slightly off, as though the original had been drawn from memory.
—Jonathon Lumen, *The Persistence of Vision* (1999)

Pym Dark came into my office and sat opposite the potted bamboo and Seurat print. His notebook, he said, contained ideas, proposals, contingencies for a new aesthetic—although, when I saw it, these ruminations were crossed out, leaving sequences of black oblongs and irregular circles reminiscent of Morse code. What his book had once held, he said, was connected to the persistence of vision, a long-debunked theory that argued perceived motion originated from the afterimage. To muddy the situation I had been a proponent of the theory, albeit a modified version that incorporated Freud's ideas on repression.

Pym rested uneasily in the chair, unsure of where to put his feet. His thin, gangly body tried to get comfortable on the hard metal frame. His threadbare suit engulfed him, as though it were three sizes too big. He resembled a younger version of myself, an eerie manifestation of my past. But *my* past, what little I knew of it, I had to find in him. I had been stripped to the abstract, to a series of blank conceptualizations. The woman, *his* woman, was the cause—though I was still at a loss to explain why. From the desk drawer, I took out a pair of blue latex gloves and a matching surgical mask and snapped them on. "I don't want to contaminate the lens," I said, opening up an inch-square black case. "This is a delicate process that will draw out certain information. The lens will get past the effects of your unconscious repression and provide me with the truth." I thumbed his right eye open and placed the small lens on his cornea. The disc of glass was laced with my own concoction, a concentrated solution of temazepam and scopolamine. I explained that I needed to manipulate the right eye to access the left side of his brain. Here I could find the fragmented images that occurred in rare flashes of lucidity or elongated periods of paradoxical sleep.

"Doctor," Pym said, "Mother once told me that art is a figment of the intellect." He had not thought much of these words when they were originally spoken. Even months after experiencing this idea in bodily form—the woman—he was still wary of what it meant. Every now and again, he said, he could smell her faint scent: a mix of liniment oil and body salt. I speculated that this recurring sensation could be a manifestation of a hope that he would see her again or as a symptom of his condition.

Following another unsuccessful semester at Harvard, he had taken the train to New York to stay with a high school friend, Kristofer L., a graduate student at Columbia. His family was from the Balkans, the borderlands between Croatia and Serbia. Pym envisioned Manhattan as the ideal place to develop his theory of aesthetics during the summer break. Years before, he had visited with his mother to take in the sights and they had stayed in a shoebox hotel near Times Square. They had seen the Statue of Liberty and a man heave on one of the pedestal walls. The man tried to scrape the vomit off with a branch, but he left odd markings that resembled a cave painting: a bison or an auroch.

In Kristofer's one-bedroom walk-up in Morningside Heights, Pym slept on the couch. For the first week he rarely left the building. He filled his time lounging in Kristofer's plush leather recliner, smoking his friend's Ronhill Whites and drinking his delicious Franck coffee. Leafing through immunology textbooks from the living room shelf, he discovered a book he had never read: a paperback edition of *Le Temps Retrouvé*. The cover bore an Impressionist watercolor of an alleyway. A fine painterly light ran through the image; the dabs of color offered him a level of decipherment, for he loved patterns, seeking them in everything. False positives, apophenia—of and in—the world were not his concern. Connections, he reasoned, existed in the ethereal and in the mundane. When it came to Proust's writing, he knew the deductions and inferences would be of a higher order. But he challenged himself to get through the four-hundred pages in one or two sittings. When he took a break from reading, he would look out onto the street and watch the comings-and-goings of a busy Jewish deli and a nineteen-seventies-era hair salon.

By the second week, Kristofer had set for Pym a new schedule: at nine, he would leave the apartment to catch the D train to Bryant Park. Then he walked one block to the Public Library. That building, Kristofer said, would be a distraction-free and scholarly location where Pym could write down his theories. Pym was glad for the change as he had not gotten past the opening section of Proust's novel—the style of the writing, the dense stream-of-consciousness, compounded by the French, prevented him from making any serious progress.

Most days he was first in line at the main entrance. Now and again an elderly man with a short graying beard and a white shirt lashed with faded black suspenders stood near the steps, studying the patterns of dried gum that littered the pavement. Pym leaned against the low wall facing the library and pretended to read the *Daily News*. The man ran his finger over the bumps and petrified tooth marks. When security opened the doors, the man wouldn't move; he didn't seem interested in what was inside. He was only focused on drawing imaginary lines from one piece of gum to another. This man was like him, a surveyor of the invisible. So one morning he sat beside him on the steps and pointed to a headline in his newspaper.

"Odd that," he said.

"What?"

"This phrase: 'Double Bind Receives Grant.' "

"I don't trust words," the man said, standing up. He paced around in a circle, making sure to avoid the gum. "Give me your coffee."

Pym felt sorry for him. They were not similar after all. The man's shirt cuffs had thick dirt rings and his pants had large ketchup stains near the crotch. Pym plucked three one-dollar bills from his wallet and offered them. "This should be enough."

"No, your cup." The man snatched it from Pym, removed the lid, and poured the coffee on the ground in a strange zigzag motion. Geometric shapes—crumpled trapezoids and wonky parallelograms—were set off from one another like a child's version of the Nazca Lines. They both stared at the patterns until the lines evaporated a few seconds later. Pym gestured that he was going inside, but the man ignored him, his focus still on the ground.

On the third floor, through marble hallways that smelled of Clorox, was Room 315. People knew it as the Rose Reading Room, a century-old area built for public consumption. As Pym entered he liked to look at the ceiling, marveling at the three murals of swirling pink clouds and light blue skies. Below, a line of offices and help desks divided the room. Each side was a fractured mirror image with slight, almost imperceptible differences. Both had rows of oak tables with brass reading lamps and leather-bound reference books stationed at the ends.

He sat at the tenth desk, on the right-hand side. He preferred it because the sunlight stayed there longest, from morning to late evening. The corner position suited his wish that everything should be in front of him. He laid out his notebook and pencils, making sure to cover the 369 on the desk as the multiples made him uneasy. During the day tourists visited; they snapped pictures and exited sharply, leaving the room in silence. Their appearance and abrupt disappearance usually went unnoted; only when they spoke loudly and their voices reverberated in wild echoes did they receive a cold stare or a roll of the eyes from an annoyed patron. One time he heard a woman complain that: "Non-members are moving the books." He could only see a sliver of her jacket, the rest of her obscured by a tour group. Her voice, though, sounded familiar as if he had heard it before in the coffee shop near the library, or back at Harvard, or from the strange years of his childhood. When the group left the woman was no longer there, and a burly attendant, who twirled his finger in the air, said, "Ten minutes. We close in ten minutes."

Like always, Pym wrote until the last second. His ideas were not constructed in the normal sense; instead he relied upon a series of repeated descriptions, one replacing another with only infinitesimal changes. These passages of text were only approximations of intent, word-images that signified the crux of his theory: enlightenment through repetition. He didn't relate his strange ideas to Kristofer, relying, as he did, on his generosity and the contents of his icebox. Pym was unsure of what his friend sought in repayment, apart from a signed copy of the treatise. It was possible, I deduced, that Kristofer thought more fondly of their years together in high school or that he empathized over the health of Pym's mother.

As the days passed at the library, Pym saw a repeating pattern of people. None of them knew each other by name, but they created a community separate from the tourists with its own space and code of nods and shrugs. A silver-haired Korean woman in dress pants and a dark peplum blazer would sit two desks away. She carried a black notebook in which she worked on an art monograph for an exhibition at the Met. On the table she would flatten 10x12 photographs of naked men and women stretched, hung, crushed, and ripped apart—the bodies bruised and tattooed with khafs, dalets, and gimels. He recognized these Hebrew letters from a linguistics class taken sophomore year, but the purpose of their placement eluded him.

The second member of his triad was a man distinguished by his pin-stripe pants and starched Yale Blue shirt. He would arrive at midday and take a seat close to the dictionary chained to the lectern. He always had with him a thick sheaf of paper and a mechanical pencil, a barrel of spare lead at the ready. On the quarter hour, he took the list of words he had been jotting down for the previous few minutes and looked them up, scrupulously writing down their meanings. Once, as Pym passed the man's desk, he found a fragment left behind: *diactinism, diad, diadelphous*.

He wasn't sure of the significance or what exactly the project entailed. The first word had something to with physics and the sending of radioactive waves; the second, usually spelled with a Y, concerned the unification of a man and a woman; and the third referred to plants—in particular, the joining of stamens. Three branches of investigation: physics, sociology, biology. The words encompassed a compendium of knowledge and lexicography, and originated from Greek and related Latin roots pertaining to the idea of two-ness. The purpose, though, remained obscure. It occurred to him that the man was a college professor on sabbatical or an academic crank completing his magnum opus.

Unlike his classes, the man's investigations inspired Pym to learn more about the nature of intellectual inquiry. He began to speculate more deeply on what the man was doing, that the words were connected to the Korean woman's project. His obsession became more malevolent and he ripped random pages from the dictionary and hid them in the book-shelves. His behavior reminded me of one of Freud's early cases, and I double-checked Frampton's *Methodologica* to aid my analysis. I compared notes with a report on Mathilde Schleicher, an Austrian woman, who suffered from erratic episodes of hysteria and melancholia. Her periods of mania would foment multiple delusions and she would exhibit paranoiac bluster, accusing Freud of preventing her from becoming the lead singer at the Vienna Opera and then of him writing her lewd villanelles. He treated her with intermittent doses of chloral hydrate and vials of bromide and morphine. In his book, Frampton held Freud responsible for her death. He noted: "In her final months, she developed a crippling somatic disease. It was reported that on her deathbed her mind had split, diverged into two separate entities—two separate women." Dwelling on the connections between Pym and Mathilde, I watered the bamboo and pulled out the dead shoots. "The plant's dying," he said. I'm not sure these were his exact words as soon after, when he noticed the tape recorder underneath my paperwork, he convinced me to delete the tape before he would continue his account.

Pym searched the library shelves in hope of finding a suitable text. Sorting through books on literature, history, and visual art, he found a four-volume set half-hidden by a wooden cart stacked with dusty encyclopedias. The books were first editions, vellum-bound with gilt spines. Each cover had a similar illustration on the front: an amphora patterned with a geometric shape—circle, triangle, square, pentagon—and the title *In Hope We Find This Nation*. Written by an Englishman, Edward Lawrence, the books detailed his personal account of New York after the First World War. Volume one contained a scant biographical note: his birth year (1894) and the fact that, after his wife died from influenza, he had traveled to America on the *USS Plattsburg* with the returning soldiers. In New York, wary of the recent subway accidents he had read of in the newspapers, he explored the city by foot and wrote in his notebook a lengthy description of the Model T Ford, the prices of bread and whiskey, unusual restaurant names (speculating on the types of food that Etaoin or Shrdlu sold), details from a Ringling Brothers billboard, and generous observations on parts of the city inhabited by the Irish, the Jews, the Chinese, and the Italians. He collected items in his buckskin satchel, often completely filling it with bus tickets, medicinal salves, political pamphlets, auction catalogues, slick magazines, almanacs, flowery poetry chapbooks (including the sordid volume, the *Meanderings of Memory*), and stereographs of the Flatiron Building and the Statue of Liberty. During the late evenings, he rested in a Bowery flophouse and wrote up his findings.

Within an hour, Pym had read the first chapter. The prose had an ornate style that let sentences go for pages, clause upon clause building an interior structure that mimicked an adding machine's computations. The material drove him on so fast he didn't notice the tears until they hit the page. He told me the pain started as a slight irritation in his left eye, a feeling that a shard of glass was scratching at his sclera, slowly peeling it off in thin strips. Saline eye drops from a nearby drugstore temporarily soothed the discomfort and allowed him to continue reading. My initial note had this down as incidental, but as he explained the subsequent events of that day I changed my opinion to something more unsettling.

In the library he found the lights flickering in an odd sequence of short and long pulses, and the mix of burning white and soft yellow altered his vision, leaving a gray film over his sight. No one close to him seemed to be affected or even have noticed the phenomenon. Somewhat alarmed, he coughed loudly in the direction of the Korean woman.

She arched her body around with a dancer's grace.

"What happened to the lights?"

The woman glanced at the chandeliers and then down to the brass lamp on his table. "They look fine."

"Are you sure?"

She collected her photographs in a slipshod fashion, roughly bundling them into her notebook, and moved to a table on the other side of the room.

In his peripheral vision he could see shadows with no substance, lucid shapes compressing into a dark wafer figure. A bareheaded woman in a cream halter dress emerged near the center of the room, but close to the exit, and her gaze was fixed on him. He considered that she was the same woman he had heard complain days before, that she preferred to sit on the other side, where she pursued a similar project to him. He closed his eyes and counted to three. On reopening them she had been replaced by the attendant, who studied Pym, and the Korean woman, who whispered in the attendant's ear and pointed Pym's way.

* * *

The hair salon opposite Kristofer's apartment had a strange name. The rusting sign, and the photographs of women in the window, reminded Pym of a typical Lawrence experiment in which he would collect business names and list them to resemble a Surrealist poem. He repeated the name over and over. Something inherent in A CUT IN TIME wouldn't leave him alone. It contained remnants of Proust, unstable memories of the past. Perhaps as a diversion he told me the hair salon was populated with a clientele different from the deli next door. The deli attracted a working crowd from the local insurance office and the strip of franchise stores half a block away. The salon entertained middle-aged women with graying hair hidden under hats and scarves. They left with colorful bobs, blond high-lights on straightened hair, or bouncy, energetic perms.

After hours of staring, the view became a postcard: a solidified image of what he imagined was outside. His attention to the scene, to the piqued detail of ordinary life, was a hangover from his indulgence in the printed word. For the old magazines and newspapers Kristofer owned soon ran out, though a vintage *New Yorker* had held Pym's attention as he attempted to decipher a story titled, "Symbols and Signs." Yet even after he attempted to translate *Le Temps Retrouvé*, with his poor French, he still had too much time to think about the woman at the library and the work of Edward Lawrence. Even when Kristofer or his girlfriend, Anya, would talk to Pym, he only half-listened.

"You know I like having you around," Kristofer said. "But it's not good for either of us to have you sit here all day."

"There's an interesting view."

Kristofer went to the window and peered outside. "So come on, what happened?"

"Writer's block."

Kristofer turned, wearily loosening his necktie, and kicked the recliner with the tip of his brogue. "That's crap. It's been a week. I have exams coming up, and Anya's complaining about your shit."

Slightly shaken, Pym stood and positioned himself between Kristofer and the collection of wine bottles, yellowing newspapers, and coffee cups with cigarette butts sunken at the bottom. He said, "I don't see what the problem is."

"You were always like this, even in honors English."

"Like what?"

"Blind to what's going on."

"That's unfair."

Kristofer picked up one of the cups and glimpsed inside. "I'm trying to help."

Pym edged past him to the window and craned his neck to see the tall buildings of Midtown. "I'll go back tomorrow."

* * *

The next day, he didn't see the woman. Maybe he had imagined her or maybe she had been another tourist, another chance meeting given too much significance. For years he had believed in coincidence. As a child he wrote his own horoscopes, changing his sign to fit with what happened the day before, and then showing the typed and dated columns to his friends as proof. Often they told their parents, and he was invited to dinner to talk about his strange gift. He never accepted the offers, though, choosing to spend his nights pasting the horoscopes into his scrapbook and reflecting on what he would write the next day.

These memories were soon lost to the business of the reading room and the familiar faces of the Korean lady and the man with his lists of words. Pym claimed his usual seat and placed his bookbag down and retrieved volume one of Lawrence's book. Several of the chapters had been dog-eared and paragraph-long annotations were scrawled in the margins. The penmanship was fine and the looped cursive writing masked what the words said. His finger traced over the lines, the odd flourishes on the F's and M's convincing him the sentences were written in code.

Chapter Two concerned an analysis of Crow Hill in Brooklyn and its change to Crown Heights in 1916. Lawrence detailed the names of the Jewish families to chart any future diaspora to another neighborhood. As a self-taught historian and linguist, he wanted to compare the situation to his own observations in England. The ensuing chapters revisited this data in unusual ways; a red ink graph displayed surname length on the x-axis and years in the neighborhood on the y. A common name like Miller corresponded to 16 years, whereas Auerbach had 22.5 years. In his conclusions, farther on, he found a disturbing correlation. Tables of data supported one hypothesis: residents were being forcibly purged. On a topographical map, an elliptical curve pinned the St. Ignatius Church as point O. The tenement buildings and brownstones were repossessed, or leases terminated, the land bought up by a fronted property company, Allmen Inc., located in Weehawken, New Jersey.

He read all day to finish the book, eating only a granola bar from his bag and taking a few sips of water from the fountain. He considered Lawrence's views, but was unsure whether to believe them. Lawrence was looking for patterns, a way to understand the world in front of him. Pym believed in Lawrence's findings, almost obsessively. Each subsequent book was longer—undoubtedly denser—and he was eager to get through them. At the shelf volume two was missing, and he examined the surrounding books to see if it had been misplaced. He ran his fingers over dozens of spines until he saw the woman from before. She was sitting on a small wooden stool, reading a book. The late afternoon light revealed a shading of gray in her hair, which seemed shorter than the previous time, as if she had received a buzz cut in the last few days. She was wearing a beige cotton cardigan over a cream vest and stonewash jeans with black pumps.

He rounded the cart and stood next to her, deciding what he should say. She was not conventionally beautiful like the girls he had dated in the past, trust fund types who were only interested in living the same lives as their parents.

She glanced up. "Are you O.K.?"

"That book you're reading," he said, pointing at it. "I'm reading the entire set—"

"And you thought that gave you priority."

"Something like that."

She dog-eared her current page and rose as if to leave. "When I've finished," she said, "I'll be sure to let you know."

He grabbed her arm and then just as quickly let it go. "No, I need it. My time is limited."

She gestured for Pym to come with her, and they went to his table. "I believe this is where you were sitting." She thrust the book down. "We need a contract," she continued. "Not a legal one. More an understanding that we should discern our reasons for reading these books."

He nodded, but was unsure of what she meant.

She pointed to the chairs. They both sat, allowing the contract to begin.

* * *

151

Through June they read together. Her clothes barely changed, just slight color variations on the same vest and jeans. On Fridays, though, she wore plain muslin dresses and wedge sandals. She smuggled in a cup of herbal tea that smelled of peppermint and lemon and she would sip it languidly, making it last the entire day. Only rarely would they talk. Occasionally there would be a stuttered conversation in which he attempted to make a date with her at a café or at the movies. She would lean in, and he could smell a hint of perfume that had been sprayed on days before. "This is our place," she would reply to his suggestions.

Following these obtuse statements, she would leave and come back days or sometimes weeks later. He wondered if she was married, and he often looked for a band of white skin or an indentation from a recently removed wedding ring. In their brief talks, she never mentioned anybody else or that she had to go and meet a friend. He often toyed with romantic notions of who she was and why she read with him. He hypothesized, feasibly, she didn't live in the city but commuted in when she was able. One early evening, when the library was full of people trying to escape the humidity, he decided to track her as she left. He gave her a couple of minutes then grabbed his bookbag and headed for the main exit. As he ran down the stairs he saw her from the window, her thin body visible as a strong breeze tightened the back of her sundress. His face pressed to the glass and he thought of calling to her, but he didn't know her name. He knew nothing about her. He could only watch as she disappeared into the crowds heading toward Grand Central.

* * *

A few weeks later, Pym and Kristofer were in a Midtown coffee shop. They had stopped there briefly at Pym's suggestion. Kristofer's foot tapping signaled to Pym that Kristofer was annoyed that he had brought him away from his studies. Pym recalled his mother's jittery hands and her telling him how caffeine eased her headaches. "They're caused by my medulloblastoma," she had said. "It's a type of brain tumor." The magnitude of what she was saying took a second to sink into Pym's mind. Before he could reply, she took his hand and squeezed the fleshy part of his palm. "How's school?"

"Take this," said Kristofer, passing Pym a cup of coffee. He offered his thanks, and they walked to the rear entrance of the library. They drank the coffee and went inside. Mirroring Pym's lead, Kristofer passed his bag to security. As the guard rummaged through the textbooks and the latest issue of *Nature*, Kristofer turned to Pym: "What are we doing here?"

"I need you to see her."

"I knew this was about a girl."

Pym didn't speak, but directed him to the stairwell.

Kristofer slung his bag over his shoulder. "Are you stalking her?"

"I haven't seen her in ages."

In Room 315, he guided Kristofer to his desk. They sat for a moment watching the archway. He pointed out the man with his wordlists; he had two bound folios of completed work and a thick sheaf ready to be inscribed. Far to his right, the Korean lady was hunched over her desk. She was editing the galleys of her monograph, noting typos and errant commas. It was difficult to see her work, though it must have been nearing completion.

Pym's odd bits of commentary bored Kristofer. To mask the time Pym showed him Lawrence's books, but he displayed no interest. "There's science in here, too," Pym said, pointing to a histogram that compared heights of city buildings. "Singer Tower, the Metropolitan Life Tower, the Woolworth—"

Kristofer stood. "I have to leave."

"Stay one more hour."

He shook his head. "Try working on those theories of yours."

For the rest of the day Pym went through his notebook, blotting out all of his sentences. In our short time together I tried to decipher a handful of the words, and I pointed to a slew of them on the page. This led to questions, though he asked them of me: *Why do you insist that I fill out a child's connect-the-dots drawing? Why are you so obsessed by Edward Lawrence? Why did you offer me money to visit your office?*

I rose from my chair and shuttered the blinds, cutting out the view of the cold storage warehouse and the outline of Manhattan beyond. He complained about the darkness and the needling sting in his right eye. I wondered if he had read Goethe's *The Theory of Colors*, a scientific treatise that ruminated on the effects of light on people. As an experiment,

I told him the blinds were not shut. That, in fact, he just imagined they were. He became quiet, and his eyes closed, as though he were meditating. I retrieved my camera from the drawer and snapped his picture, and although later the negatives were destroyed in the darkroom, he remained unaware of my actions. I told him I would open the blinds, if he abandoned his questions and continued.

He shaded his eyes with his hand, and I saw him take in the gold shine of the nameplate on my desk. "Dr. Phot, please. I agree."

His past attempt in trailing her led—although he was not sure how—to a prolonged absence on her part, and as the summer wore on he read by himself. In volume three, he found a lengthy description of the changing color of the Hudson River. Lawrence observed the water shift from a grayish blue at dawn to a blackened orange at sunset. Over a two-month period, he became enamored with the river and spent much of his time observing the fishing boats putter in and out of the harbor. In late September of 1920, he acquired passage on an aging sailing trawler that had been hired to transport scientific instruments to Troy. On the hurried journey upriver, he often wondered about the crate locked in the hold. It didn't seem worthwhile to take such a small cargo. His queries to the captain went unanswered, and this fueled his paranoia about what they were really carrying. For days he speculated in his notebook: a cache of forged Liberty bonds. Photographs of women in unnatural states. A dismembered body.

As the trawler passed Cortlandt, he found the hold open. He examined the crate, noting the same Allmen Inc. stamp he had seen on the mortgage documents in Crown Heights. Before he could peek inside, the cook discovered him and Lawrence was confined to his cabin. He was given a bed, a wooden slop bucket, and his trunk, which contained his second set of clothes (short suit jacket and cuffed trousers, waistcoat, and tan leather belt) and a book of matches, which he lit to make crude charcoal. He used his captivity to sketch the landscape he could see through the porthole. As the ship neared Troy his drawings of the low hills and the maple and cedar forests became otherworldly, branches elongated across the whole sky. He remained in the makeshift brig for two days. After his release in Troy, he put his visual madness down to a type of parasiticide poisoning. He returned to New York by train convinced his sickness had originated from the river, his drinking water tampered with by the crew.

Pym studied the facsimile reproductions of the drawings. Several pages were a smudged mess, a conglomeration of black lines merging into one another as though white space needed to be eliminated. It reminded him of his failed attempt to describe a new aesthetic, a system of explicating the abstract from the unreal. Since his mother's cancer had worsened, he had not been able to see her face; his memories of her lost to another time. He stared at the drawings all of the afternoon, trying to mentally reassemble the lines into a close approximation of her face.

* * *

At a later point, Pym recounted, he attended a movie club situated at the north end of Central Park that played old black-and-white films using a 16mm projector and a white tarpaulin pinned to the side of Belvedere Castle. Run in secret by organizers in balaclavas and thick woolen jackets, the men played avant-garde montages of porcine copulation and ironclad warships maneuvering into dry dock. Other films had Chinese women pointing to their foot binding and then a brutal cut to the open sea, cloudless to the horizon. Each film ended with a serene visage: calm water, clear sky, a painted wall. Like a Rorschach test, the films provoked different interpretations, new ways for the audience to understand what was going on. He intuited a system at work, something dynamic and overarching. The image of the boar mounting the sow existed for shock value; the close up of the penis intercut with the warship closing in on the dock was almost a pastiche of the nineteen-fifties conditioning films he studied in his psychology classes.

Several times he considered not going back, but instead reinstating his trips to the library. Yet the cloying mystery of the club and the hurried manner of the organizers—who stripped the equipment down and dashed out of the park—kept him interested. One night he watched from behind a ginkgo tree, a pocket telescope aiding his view. They erected the impromptu cinema in less than half an hour, using ropes and a pulley to hoist the tarpaulin and a crate on a park bench to support the projector. The film started with a lion dying from an epileptic fit, the body shaking on the floor of a circus cage. A crude splice transitioned to a grass field. At the edge of the screen he could see the girl from the library naked. She wore a coarse wig, resembling theatrical hair. He wasn't sure what to make of the image or even feel able to clearly assess whether it was her captured on those reels of celluloid.

Realizing he had to act, he crept up on the man packing the projector away and yanked off his balaclava. The man's face was sweaty, his beard unkempt, and he looked around the park as if people would identify him and call the police.

"Who is she?"

The man stepped away. "I don't know."

"How did you get her picture?"

"These are the things we do," he said.

* * *

The day before Pym was to return to Harvard he found her at his desk, reading the last book. He approached, attempting to be casual, with one hand in the front pocket of his jeans and the other loosely holding his sunglasses. As they made eye contact she didn't speak, but pointed to where she was on the page.

He put his hand on her shoulder. "I want to see you outside."

"We can only be together here in this room."

"But why?" he said, taking his hand away so that he could cross his arms. "I don't understand."

"You don't need to."

"I saw you in a film," he said.

"You're mistaking me for someone else."

"You were naked."

"Do you really think that's likely?"

"I don't know."

"Let's read."

Volume four concerned Lawrence's self-imposed containment and his continued sickness, which now consisted of muscle cramps in his legs and arms and severe headaches throughout the day. He kept within ten blocks of the flophouse, fearing the rivers on either side of the island. One morning, while he strolled through the neighborhood, a tourist took his picture outside of an Italian café that served cannoli and strong coffee for a nickel. *He wondered why he had been in the picture: Had his illness been apparent? Or was the man just interested in the picturesque frontage of the café?*

Over the winter these questions troubled him more as he saw the growth of photography in the city, particularly the underground trend of solarisation. While in the darkroom prints would be subjected to blazing bursts of light, altering the tone, the lines of contrast, and the sharp gradations of the shadows. The images, according to Lawrence, were absurd. Models were rendered androgynous—flesh disappeared into the ether. He remarked upon the exhibitions circulating through Paris, London, and New York: "Light—Visions," "Dada: The Magic Binary," and "City/Gray/Space." He learned about decalomania and frottage and he became haunted by ghostly rayographs, like the imprint of a wire-coil on a sheet of photosensitive paper. At his lodgings he set up a darkroom, buying equipment from a bankrupt camera club. At night he roved the streets and snapped pictures of Lower East Side prostitutes. Often they posed for him, sometimes clothed, sometimes not. Rarely did they charge him. While developing a later batch of negatives he decided to attempt his own solarisations on the forthcoming prints, but the images came out gray and muddy. For almost a year he worked on the process, slowly getting closer to an untainted photograph. He used different light sources: a flashlight, a candle, a flare, a carbide lamp. All failed. Only an editor's postscript indicated what happened next. Lawrence had abandoned the flophouse, owing six months of rent. His writings, sketches, photographs, and clothes were found by the landlady and sold and later ended up with a publisher based in New Jersey.

The woman tired of the accumulation of facts, events, and observations. She flipped the pages with a listless pace. Her eyes were sunken, and her skin had grown visibly pale. He wasn't sure, as they read in silence, if this was related to the film or his presence being anathema to her health. He knew as she came to the last page, he needed to break the impasse: "I leave tomorrow."

She pointed to the sentence she was on.

"I have my answer," he lied.

"I'm sad it's over." She closed the book.

"I thought we could read something else. I see now why that wouldn't work." He got up and collected his things.

* * *

That afternoon was the only juncture of this strange episode in which I saw Pym. I palmed him a check for an amount that could pay for an Upper East Side divorce. He studied it and told me to rip it in half. He suspected that I was the man in the park, the gum man, the man with his wordlists, even Kristofer L. He said I was an actor and called me Garrick and Stanislavski. I realized for hours he had been talking, projecting his fantasies onto me—like the word-images he had sought in his theories.

Still, I wanted to know more. I needed more information: a way for me to get Lawrence's books. Discovering these missing volumes accorded me a chance to return to my old life or, at least, what I remembered of it: a wife and a daughter. If, as Pym said, I were acting, I envisaged it as more caught in a performance—not just of a text, but of an existence. Pym's experiences were the route to recovering my own sense of memory, and I offered him anything he wanted. He pointed to the Seurat.

"It is yours," I said.

"And this?" he said, pointing to his right eye.

I sized him up, tipped his head back, and with a cotton swab coaxed the lens from his cornea. His pupil looked milky, as though it had been damaged by the procedure. I stood to the side, allowing him to rise and lift the print off the wall. He leaned it against my desk, and he went to the window and scissored the blinds with two of his fingers.

"And the rest?" I pled.

At the Christmas break, Kristofer invited Pym to watch the apartment while he visited his family in Vukovar. He hesitated at first, unsure if he wanted to relive the strange events of the summer. He went, though, taking the same train as before. Kristofer's place was close to how he remembered it, only cleaner and with a new chrome bookcase shaped like a wave and filled only with textbooks. Kristofer had stored enough food in the icebox to last for a few days: cold cuts—mostly pastrami and corned beef—a bag of Cortland apples, a fresh carton of skim milk, two loaves of wheat bread, and several cans of tuna. The supplies came with a note, held down by a bacterium-shaped fridge magnet, which had instructions for living in the apartment and, underneath, a pamphlet detailing the library's opening hours over the holidays.

For a long spell he stared out of the window, taking in the view now dashed with a cold gray sludge, and drank vermouth mixed weakly with tonic. Through the warm haze of the alcohol he thought of his mother, who had died a month or so before. His last day with her had gone poorly; she barely knew Pym. She instructed him, though, after Pym told her of his summer experiences, to appreciate truth in all of its forms. He left the hospital unsure what to do with her advice, but in New York he had to know if the woman still visited the library. After sleeping on these considerations, he took the subway to Times Square and exited past the heavy crowds shopping for gifts, to East 42nd, toward the Chrysler Building. He waited in Bryant Park, shivering in the cold wind and rain, and stared at the library until the doors opened with a muffled thud. He headed up the marble steps, past Corinthian columns, and into the cool, quiet interior. He drifted through corridors and anterooms, switching floors by winding staircases, without fully realizing where he was going.

On the third floor, a stuffy heat from the vents and a swirling breeze from the windows had replaced the summer air. A large notice on the wall detailed an upcoming restoration: sections of the library would be closed one by one, refurbished, then reopened in the same sequential order. A footnote at the bottom indicated the Rose Reading Room would be the first to undergo the process. The tables and chairs would be taken out and polyethylene sheets laid down; the books would also be removed to an underground chamber.

The Korean lady and the wordlist man were gone, substituted by a new triad: the NYU student cramming for his finals, the panhandler by the heater, and the bored library clerk staring out from his booth. Pym searched for Lawrence's books, but once he found them missing he asked the clerk if he could locate them. *In Hope We Find This Nation*, the clerk said, had been deposited into storage due to its low circulation rate and wouldn't be available until after the restoration.

"But here," he said, "here is the light."

CPSIA information can be obtained at www.ICGtesting.com
Printed in the USA
LVOW10s2003110815

449711LV00006B/249/P